THE WHENS OF
WICK

BLUE BOX BOOKS

THE WHENS OF WICK
RETURN OF THE WICK CHRONICLES
BOOK ONE

Published by Blue Box Books
www.blueboxbooks.com

ISBN 978-1-932461-56-5

Printed in the United States of America

THE WHENS OF
WICK

*To Tad, who would
save Wick every time...*

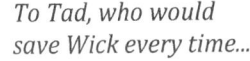

RETURN OF
THE WICK CHRONICLES
BOOK ONE

There was a gentleness to Will's married life that tugged on my furry little heartstrings. He woke every morning at stupid o'clock to either run with Jax around Union Square or to hit the gym or the pool. Sometimes he ran with Drew; they looped the Square a few times before heading for the university, and then Will ran home alone. Most mornings he slipped out of bed at four-thirty and was back and showered by the time Aisha was awake and Jay was scrambling to get out the door and to his first class.

He did it because he felt like he owed the people he loved and who loved him back the best of himself. I didn't mind his early-morning efforts because he rarely woke me to go with him; when he did wake me it was unintentional, and I occasionally wanted to go even if it was WTF o'clock. Sometimes I sat on a step on Union Square and watched him run with Jax, and I might or might not have yelled *run faster* a few times. But most of the time I stayed inside, curled up at the foot of the bed, and waited for Aisha to wake up.

After he showered, he almost always made breakfast for his family. It gave Aisha time to nurse a mug of herbal tea while she tried to wake up enough to go to work, and gave Jay time for last minute studying while he shoveled his food in.

Will never let Jay—whom he'd known for years as Zed's best friend Jimmy without realizing that he was the son of the woman whose heart he had broken—leave home without hearing that he was loved, and he never let Aisha leave without a kiss and the whispering of mushy things that made her smile. Without saying so, he wanted to be sure that if something happened during the hours they were apart, that they knew, without a doubt, that they were the breath that allowed his heart to keep beating. What he wanted least was to ever part on a cross word or an ill feeling.

"If the worst came to be," he told me when I asked why it mattered to him so much, "I would not want the final words I said to the people who matter most to be things I would take back if I could. I want the last thing they hear from me to be kind, and I don't want the last things we feel to be angry and haunting."

'If I had known the last time was going to be the last time, it would not have been the last time.' Like that?

"That's very astute, Wick."

King Eli said that once. He was a little bit drunk and missing his queen. He wished for one more moment to tell her he loved her.

Eli's last words to Queen Donna had been of his love. Assured that she had another day, possibly two, he told her he loved her and would be back in an hour. She had plans of her own; she didn't want him to see her draw her last breath. She didn't want the last moments of her life to be etched onto his soul, the sound of her last breath leaving her body to be the thing he would remember most. He left the room and she watched him go, then she smiled at Jax, exhaled, and was gone.

Eli's regret was bound tightly with the order of his words. If he could take it back, he would first tell her that he'd return soon, and leave her with love being the last thing to drip from his tongue. No one could convince him that she'd heard what she needed to: she owned his heart and that he would see her again.

Aubrey believed that. She held him while he grieved, trying to dull the edges off the worst of his pain, and reminded him that he would be with her again one day. When he'd lived out the days he was allotted, his reward for a life lived well would be the rest of forever with her.

He didn't believe that quite as strongly as she did, but he tethered hope to her faith and told himself she was right.

Will didn't want to feel that kind of regret. He knew that accidents sometimes happened and that time might decide to devour him because he remained where he didn't belong, so he made sure that the words he said before parting mattered, even if they were simple and softly spoken.

His entire life was exceptionally more settled than it had been before Aisha walked into his birthday party, the celebration of him reaching forty-three, an age he had never expected to see. He no longer had to fight against the cruelty of being displaced, time picking at him like a scab, oozing disquiet and robbing him of rest. He didn't have the certain promise of death hanging over him, because he'd survived his own expiration date. When the world didn't end two hundred years in the future, and he didn't lose the thing that keeps him anchored in this When—me—his existence became something he embraced rather than something he was trying to get through.

He lived, he was with the love of his life, he was months away from becoming a father, and he rejoiced in the gentle joy that Aisha had brought into his world.

She was his anchor as much as I was, and for that I was grateful. I watched him sleep next to her, his hand splayed out over her still-flat belly—they hadn't told anyone other than Jay, and I was sworn to silence—and felt a surge of warm fuzzies that could only be explained as gratitude.

Or it could have been gas.

Never discount the possibility that it's gas.

I curled up on the window seat in their bedroom. Something was tickling the back of my brain, whispering words I couldn't hear. I did what Aubrey had once told Oz and Zed to do when they declared they were too old to have someone sit next to them for bedtime prayers: she asked them to recite the blessings in their lives, and to drift off to sleep with the wonderful gifts they'd been given being the last things they thought about at night.

I had a long list. I thought I'd fall asleep before I got to them all, but that was all right. There was always the next night and the night after that. It could take me weeks to touch on all the good things life had given me.

I closed my eyes and started with the people closest to me.

Will, always Will. He now had Aisha and a baby on the way. He was a stepfather to Jay, who had once been Jimmy but traded it for a more grown-up name, and Jay loved him as much as he did his own father. Will slept more and laughed a lot; he was content, which made me happy. He had another anchor, which gave me peace.

Oz and Drew had gotten married. Their commitment to forever was made official on New Year's Eve in Grace Cathedral, with 600 guests watching inside and thousands more viewing the ceremony on massive monitors outside and around the city. After a honeymoon split between Will's birth When and (as new adults do) Disneyland, they settled into domestic bliss, living in Oz and Zed's old bedrooms—Jax blew the wall out between them, which he enjoyed doing far more than he would admit to, so much that Aubrey worried he'd find other walls to knock down—while they both went to school and studied history and science and plotted the path their lives together would follow. Drew and Will launched Ozoo Enterprises and were already on their way to making Elysium a reality. Drew understood me, he heard my words and not just my voice, and he cared about me as much as Will and Jax did. If I ever needed an anchor of my own, Will was certain Drew could be the person I needed.

King Eli came home. He'd accepted Jax's offer (Jax begged, but still) to serve as Pacifica's representative to the Consortium and he spend his time lobbying other representatives to allow Florida entry into the offshoot of the United Nations. He was invigorated by the work, which made Jax twenty kinds of happy, and even though Eli could be abrupt, he was fun and funny, and I liked having him around. He'd claimed Will as his own, and in turn claimed Jay as his grandson. That made me happy because Jay had never known what it was like to have a grandparent, and Eli wasn't going to let that go on. He insisted on Jay calling him "Grandpa," which tripped up Oz and Zed because they'd always called him "granddad" and had no idea he hated it.

"That was your grandmother's doing," he explained. "She thought it sounded more dignified. I don't want to be dignified, I want to be your grandpa."

He was going to be granddadpa for a while.

Zed was the happiest I'd ever known him to be. Sophia Lopez moved here with the excuse of getting an education, but the truth is that she came to be with Zed. She made him want to be better, and part of his personal growth was an increasing willingness to cater to my whims. Zed still wanted his castle; when he was little he wanted it because he was a prince, and why not? He wanted it now because Sophia deserved the creative side of him, and he could see it as a unique home one day. The important thing, though, was that he was becoming a kind person. He had always been able to sniff out what a person was feeling—literally—but now instead of mocking them for it, he used it to offer support. He was gradually taking on Aubrey's traits of empathy. If he stayed on the path he'd stepped onto at fourteen, he would become a formidable voice for the dead; Will wanted to nudge him away from that and encouraged his interest in architecture, but I still felt that looming ahead for Zed. He might build his castle one day, but it would still become a school where others were taught to speak for the dead.

And now I had Jay. He had been Zed's best friend before Will married Aisha, and now they were like brothers. Jay didn't blink at the odd truths of the Blackshear's lives; he thought Will's ability to hear inside peoples' heads was kind of a superpower. Oz and Jax's synesthesia seemed normal to him. Zed's sniffing of emotions was just another thing. *Of course* Drew and Will could understand and carry on conversations with me, and the portals were just a way to go places and see things a long time away. His life before becoming a Blackshear had been difficult and complicated; instead of making him bitter, it made him compassionate. He wasn't embarrassed to tell someone he loved them, and he was, despite his chronic abuse of the Bad Word List, a gentleman.

And there was Jax and Aubrey, the King and Queen, who loved everyone so much and so hard that, for them, letting go was almost impossible. We were their family, this was the family residence, and God help anyone who tried to pull one of us away.

I thought about all of that, the things Aubrey would say were the blessings of my life, as I drifted off.

It was a life I didn't want to let go of.

It was a life I had no idea how I'd come to have.

2

I'd gone to sleep on the window seat but woke up in the middle of Will and Aisha's bed with him pleading for me to wake up and her tears pinging off my furs. I heard him before I was completely awake, calling my name; I felt his hand on my chest, shaking me, and I tried to get my paws around the things I'd been dreaming about so that I wouldn't forget.

I'd forgotten too much in my life. If I could help it, I didn't want to forget anything else.

"Thank god," he breathed when I opened my eyes. I was on my back, paws in the air, and he was holding me down on the mattress.

Unhand my useless nipples. I never gave consent to this.

"You were screaming—"

Aisha interrupted his explanation. As he let go, she scooped me up and held me close, cradling me as she rocked back and forth. "Wick, you poor baby."

Can you save this for the pending sticky person? It's not dignified.

Will reached up to touch my chin. "Wick, you were screaming, and I couldn't wake you. It was terrifying. Let her hold you for a minute."

Fine. But why were you molesting my nipples?

"I wasn't—" He sighed. "I was trying to hear. There's no fur around your nipples, and I hoped I could reach you."

He'd never tried that before. He'd been able to understand me since he was a toddler, so there was never a need for him to listen to my thoughts. Even when he had no control, when he didn't know how to stop himself from hearing the things that people think to themselves, he hadn't peeked inside my head. I was well covered in fur, and we both assumed that was why he didn't hear me when my mouth was closed.

Did you?

"No."

Maybe try my paw pads next time. I use those when I listen to dreams. That might work.

"I would prefer there not be a next time. Do you remember what you were dreaming about?"

Stars. And falling. I was stuck somewhere that terrified me, and suddenly there were stars, and then I felt like I was falling.

Aisha finally set me down, but she kept a hand on my back, absently stroking my fur with her fingers. "Stay in bed with us, all right? I'll feel better if you're right here."

"I don't think I'll be able to get back to sleep," Will said. He slipped back under the covers anyway, and patted his chest, inviting me to curl up there. "Do you remember anything else?"

Eggs.

Rain.

The dream slipped away, even though I'd dug my claws in. I promised Will I was all right and would go back to sleep, but he was nervous and upset, and his night was over.

*

Oz hugged me. Drew hugged me. Aubrey and Jo and Jay hugged me. I was passed around like a brand new sticky person and gifted kisses on my head, and I tolerated the indignity of it because they meant well, and no one had bad breath. Jax didn't hug me because he knew how I felt about it but said that he could sympathize with me, and Eli said that he understood, too. He'd had too many dreams that ended with someone shaking him awake, and he recalled one particular dream that wasn't horrible but resulted in his Queen twisting his left nipple because it was crude, and she hadn't needed to hear about it.

No one pressed for details, which might have disappointed him a bit.

Zed felt bad for me, but he didn't try to hold me and he didn't try to empathize. He said that it sucked, and then offered me a bite of cheese before heading out to meet Sophia Lopez, who had supposedly moved to San Francisco to go to school, but who really was there because of him. She had moved here for school the same way Drew had. The university was in San Francisco; they both could have gone to any school in the world, but the people they loved and wanted to do unspeakable things to were here.

Jay tagged along with Zed—his girlfriend, Zara, lived in the same building as Sophia, three floors up, so they were going to watch a video with the apartment door open so that Zara's father wouldn't worry about *those boys*—and Eli left to go have a drink with Finn and Jo.

"Still have that bail account?" Jax asked Will. "I have a feeling you might need it when your grandfather comes to visit."

The old King, Eli, had been spending a lot of time with Finn. He missed Will's grandparents— he'd lived across the street from them in Glasgow, and Will often joked that he needed to keep the bail account open because one day they would get into trouble not easily gotten out of—but now Craig and Henryetta Ferguson were on the other side of the portals. Will had sent them to 2617 because his grandmother was nearly broken by living so far from her family and her own When. She needed to go home, and it was easier to visit in her there than in Scotland. Eli missed them but popped through the portal on Union Square often to visit, they could visit here, and Craig was planning on coming for Eli's birthday.

There would be drinking, and there would be shenanigans.

"I do," Will said. "I hadn't considered my father as part of the equation, but I suppose now I need to."

"That's a good thing, isn't it?" Aubrey patted her lap. I assumed it was for me and I jumped up, but then I thought it might have been for Jax because you never know with people. "Finn has been focused on work since he got here. If Eli can pull him out of the lab every now and then, it will make Jo happy."

"It will make her happier if he's home more often. He's doing better with that."

She goes home to the other When with him a lot. Eli sometimes goes, too. They might all get arrested in the future, and she might be the instigator.

"Indeed," Will chuckled. "And to that end, I should consider going forward to start an additional bail fund."

Aubrey mused that one should be established for Aisha if they cut her loose in the twenty-seventh century again as evidenced by a short vacation they'd taken together to celebrate Jax and Aubrey's birthdays in Will's birth When. It was a fun week, but along the way we were stalked by women who wanted DNA from Will so that they could create his clone, and Aisha threatened one of them with having bodily parts tied up that under ordinary circumstances should not be tied.

Aisha was scrappy; she'd already saved Will's life a couple of times and had tackled Jay's step-father hard enough to take him through a portal into another When, so it wasn't outside the realm of possible that she actually might tie into a knot body parts that normally could not be looped around each other.

"We might all wind up there at the same time," Jax snorted. "Better be a damn big fund."

Jax grabbed a bottle of scotch and three glasses and was surprised when Aisha declined and again when Will said to make his drink a short shot.

"I need to be able to get up at four-thirty," Will explained. "If I start drinking with you, I'll be tempted to stay in bed, and I'd miss our laps around Union Square."

"So, we skip tomorrow's run. A down day might be good."

"Is this the King's way of getting out of it? Get the Emperor drunk, so he has an excuse and isn't the one who backs out?"

Jax poured more scotch into Will's glass. "I'm tired, Will. I want to sleep in."

I'd kept Will up most of the night, so he decided skipping the next run was fine, but he wasn't getting drunk. "I know I'll have one ear open all night. Unless *you* want Wick tonight."

Hey.

"Sleep where you want," he told me. "But if you're with us, I know I'll be listening."

Just for that, I will.

"It sounds like he had night terrors," Aubrey said. "He's never had that problem, has he?"

I'm right here, people.

And no, I have not.

"I've seen him try to run in his sleep, and he's chattered and drooled, but this was the first time he's screamed. He can't remember what he was dreaming."

This is where you say, 'poor baby' and give me some cheese.

No one got up to get the cheese, so I tapped Aubrey's face with my paw.

Cheese.

Cheeeeese.

After I patted her again, right on the lips, she asked Will what it was I wanted so badly. His eyebrow ticked up just a hair, and he said, "A kiss, it seems."

She kissed the top of my head.

You're dead to me, Will.

"Stop it. You've had enough cheese tonight. If you get any more, you're definitely sleeping here with Jax and Aubrey, because I'm blocking the cat flap into our apartment."

Aubrey cuddled me even closer and stood up. "Come on, sweetheart. He didn't say you couldn't have ham, and we have some left over from dinner."

If she'd carried me just a little bit differently, I would have looked at him over her shoulder and stuck my tongue out.

3

He didn't want to get up at four-thirty, I remembered that. Jax wanted to have a drink and then sleep in, and Will agreed that taking a day off from running was a good idea, so there was no getting up at 4:30.

I patiently waited on the bed's headboard, and at 4:35 I jumped onto the mattress by his pillow.

Will.

Will.

Will.

Aisha rolled over and pulled me away from him, settling me in the space between them, where the warms that leeched off their bodies collided and made the bed nice and toasty. Any other time I would have enjoyed the warms and curled up to take a nap. "Let him sleep, sweetie."

But it's important.

"Ssh."

She drifted off again, her hand on my side. I waited long enough to be sure she'd fallen back asleep and then wiggled out from under her hand until I was near Will's head. I didn't need to get all the way onto his pillow, I only needed to get a paw on his head. He turned toward me; his eyes were darting back and forth, which meant he was dreaming, and that meant I could reach him without waking him.

With my paw on his cheek and the air from his nose fanning my whiskers, I closed my eyes and eased into his dream. It never took long to find the right spot; I slipped in and listened, then followed the soft sounds of wishes and fears. People dreamed all over their brains, but I only needed to find one spot where I could see and hear everything.

Once there, I waited at the fringe to see if he was busy being a superhero and saving damsels in distress or if he was being chased by dragons and giant three-headed babies. I didn't often catch him in dreams, but sometimes when I did he was mentally digesting incidents of childhood bullying—those were never fun—and some of the time he was running with a flaming sword in hand, chased by a fantastical monster that drooled acid and fire, though he usually woke up before he slayed anything. Deep down, he didn't want to chop the heads off monster babies any more than I wanted to see it.

Instead of there being anything exciting happening in this dream, he was sitting on a bench at the Crissy Field beach, watching ten-year-old Oz and twelve-year-old Drew tease eight-year-old Zed with cups filled with wet sand.

He watched them from behind sunglasses, but I knew he was seeing them and not their guards because he grinned, just a little bit, when Oz turned on Drew and showered him with a single wad of compacted sand that exploded from her cup and splattered against his chest and chin.

He'd lived this day twice. It was the day Levi Munson sent one of Drew's former guards to San Francisco to kill the young prince. Will had lived through the assassination and the aftermath that nearly destroyed Oz and Zed, and then through the moments when he stepped back in time to save Drew's life.

At first, I thought this was the most boring dream ever, but in a few minutes you're going to get up and sneak behind the bathroom and break someone's neck.

Dream-Will turned his head; he heard me, but he didn't see where I was.

I jumped on the bench and sat next to him to make it easier.

I didn't know you still dreamed about this.

"Every now and then," he said. "In my dream, nothing horrible happens. I simply sit here and watch them play. I quite enjoy this. My fondest days back then were spent watching them while they made each other laugh."

You can't turn it into a memory.

"I know. But dreaming about the way things should have been is comforting."

I dream about a never-ending plate of shrimp sometimes.

"Of course, you do. And not to be rude, but why are you eavesdropping on my dream tonight?"

Aisha wouldn't let me wake you up, but I really needed to talk to you before I forgot.

The beach faded from his mind, the kids' laughter thinning with the fog, and it was just the two of us on the bench in the dark, with a soft light glowing around us. "Do I need to wake up for this?"

If he stayed inside the dream, we could talk and not wake Aisha.

No. I had things in my head that I need to tell you about and it felt like it couldn't wait. There was a boy and a fountain. I think it was the one at Ghirardelli Square. He was feeding me, and the hippies tried to chase me away.

"Another bad dream?"

No, it really happened.

"A memory, then. Do you recall anything else?"

Fireworks. A nice day. I heard someone talking about a guy named Johnson being hung in effigy. I'm not sure if it all happened on the same day, though. It feels kind of jumbled up, like memory soup.

"Was the nice day cold or warm? Do you remember?"

Warmish. Some people wore t-shirts, but some people had on jackets.

"What about the boy? What do you remember about him?"

He was very pink and had short red hair. He was small like Jay was small last year. But then he wasn't. He gave me bologna until a woman told him to stop. Then he gave me kibble and was sorry it wasn't more.

"He fed you more than once, then?"

I think he fed me for a long time. He was there every day.

"Always near the fountain?"

No, I remember running along the bleachers at the aquatic park. Sometimes he was there, and he brought food. Sometimes people yelled at me. Men with newspapers sat on the bleachers and talked about Vietnam and lit their suckers on fire.

"Suckers?"

Lollipops? I don't know. They lit the ends and sucked smoke out of them. It smelled awful.

"I have to wake up now, Wick. I believe I know the rough time frame of where you were in the years before Dad found you."

I slipped out of his dream and took my paw off his head. It was another minute before his eyes fluttered open, but he was fully awake and put his finger to his mouth to make sure I would be quiet and not wake Aisha again. I didn't say anything until we were in the kitchen and he was making coffee.

When was I?

Will booted up his tablet and lid onto a stool at the breakfast bar. I sat near his elbow because unlike Jax, Aisha didn't care if I got on the counters as long as I stayed away from the food. "Johnson was president of the United States from nineteen-sixty-three to nineteen-sixty-nine," he said, poking at the tablet. "If you were at Ghirardelli Square, it had to be after it was converted from a factory, which was nineteen sixty-four."

I waited while he researched.

"Here." He pointed to the page he'd pulled up. "Johnson was hung in effigy on May twenty-second in nineteen-sixty-five as a protest against the Vietnam war. But you recall fireworks?"

Lots of them. Lots of people watching them, too.

"Given that, and the tidbit about Johnson, I think you remember July of that year. There would have been fireworks on the fourth of July."

His name was Tad.

"His name was Lyndon," Will said absently. He looked up and blinked. "Oh. You meant the boy."

Tad No. Or maybe Tad Stopit.

"Are you sure his name wasn't 'Nono Tad'?" Will asked with a chuckle.

Maybe. It also might have been Dammit Tad.

Will turned at the sound of the bedroom door creaking open. Before he could apologize for not being quieter, Aisha sighed and said, "Wick, I told you not to wake him up."

"He didn't."

She looked dubious.

"He slipped into my dream, and I woke by choice. It truly was important to him, Enzo. He remembered a specific point of time in his past and someone who was apparently taking care of him."

"Ah." She kissed the top of my head. "Still, Wick, some things can wait. He would have been awake in an hour or two on his own."

"He truly needed to discuss this and waiting would have felt torturous to him. He wanted to speak to me before he forgot."

Will you take me there?

"To see yourself several hundred years ago?"

If we can find me and find Tad, maybe we can figure out where I came from and when I was born.

"That could become complicated, Wick. Even if we find this boy, there's no guarantee he knows anything about how you came to be."

I know. But now I remember Tad, and that means someone cared for me. I need to see. I'm tired of forgetting.

"All right," he said. "It wouldn't hurt to at least go take a look around Ghirardelli and see if we can find you."

And Tad. We have to find Tad. He might know things, even if he doesn't know he knows them.

4

Aisha tried to not laugh at Will's new haircut, but it was shorter than she'd ever seen on him, and with the new clothes Mrs. Kovlov made for him he looked like he belonged in a video produced to teach bored teenagers about mid-twentieth century U.S. history. She apologized for snickering, but I don't think she meant it.

"I could get away with jeans and a sweatshirt in the mid-nineteen-sixties," he said, "but I might stick out. I certainly couldn't wear Wick's sweatshirt. I need to be able to fade into the background, and possibly look non-threatening if I need to speak with this boy."

You need those things on your face. That you look through.

"Glasses?" he asked me.

"You need to take glasses?" Aisha asked.

"Not—" He had to think for a moment. "He meant glasses for the correction of eyesight difficulties. People used to wear—"

"I know what glasses are, sweetheart," she snickered. "I'm not sure you can find any on short notice, though. Unless you want to take your sunglasses."

Sunglasses are still a thing, you know.

"I can leave you home, you know."

We would be on the tail end of the beatnik era. He could get away with tight jeans, which he usually favored, but with that came presumptions of a lifestyle he feared would generally be looked down upon by the mainstream. If he were going to simply sit somewhere and watch, he would go in jeans and a regular sweatshirt, but he worried that he'd never get close to Tad if he fit a potentially unfavorable stereotype.

"San Francisco has always been traditionally ahead of the curve when it comes to acceptance and tolerance, but that boy probably has adults around him who would jump to conclusions."

"About?" Aisha prodded.

"Drug use. Sexuality. Liberal nineteen-sixties San Francisco might seem uncomfortably constrained by our standards."

Mrs. Kovlov had designed comfortable slacks and a button-down shirt for him—things that were not much different than what he would wear with a suit, but the textiles of our When didn't exist in the 1960s and were just different enough to draw attention—and she'd created a casual jacket for him, one he could hide me in. There was an interior chest pocket that I fit into, but my presence wasn't obvious from the outside. With me there, it looked like he had a wallet tucked into his jacket. As long as I didn't squirm, no one would think twice.

"Good thing he's so small," she told Will. "Any bigger, it wouldn't work."

She never asked why he needed clothing made entirely from cotton, a textile she rarely worked with, and she didn't press him on the need to conceal me. The Emperor had a request, she was happy to fulfill it.

We started at a coffee shop near the plaza at the end of Market Street. Half of the people sitting at nearby tables were guards because Aubrey was meeting Aisha there to keep her company for the few minutes we would be gone. Locals would leave the Queen alone. They were used to her walking the streets downtown, and many of them had either been a student of hers or were parents of the ten-year-old kids she was currently teaching to multiply and divide and not eat paste, but tourists often gawked and some couldn't resist the urge to approach. Keeping guards close by wasn't just a safety issue; it allowed her some normalcy, a chance to sit with a friend and chat over coffee while the curious were kept at a distance.

"You be damned careful," Aisha told Will once she was done mocking him for his new fashion sense. "If you're not back in half an hour—"

"I'll be back. But if something delays me beyond that half hour, call Drew. Don't come after me yourself."

"Like hell."

"Enzo." He scooted closer to her and kissed her right at her temple. "Drew and Oz are killing time at the Ferry Building and can be here in a few minutes. He knows I'm going, and he knows you're here. Let him be the one to come rescue me."

"Aubrey would want to know why."

"She won't think twice if you call Drew and ask him if he wants to be my hero today. It would make sense to send him. It's sexist, but the When I'm headed to would demand it. Please. Stay here."

Should we not go? She's gonna worry the whole time, and maybe she shouldn't worry.

I thought she was staying behind because she was nauseated a lot of the time and didn't want to vomit four-hundred-fifty-two years ago. If she stayed in the coffee shop with Aubrey, she could nibble on a bagel and sip peppermint tea, and the odds were pretty good that she wouldn't hork right onto the Queen. But then she sighed and said she wished she could go with us, but she understood it would look wrong.

Why? She could get ugly clothes, too.

"It's not the clothing, Wick," Will said.

Then what?

He grimaced, just a bit. "I am pink, and she is not. All right?"

"Sweetheart, you're not really pink, either," Aisha snickered.

He didn't know of another way to explain it to me. He looked pink to me. Drew was not as pink. Aisha was less pink than either of them, but when she blushed I saw pink in her cheeks. And I had no idea why that mattered.

"There's no time to explain the history of racial divide and inequality to him. Wick just sees people. If we went together, anyone who viewed us as a couple would likely have a negative reaction."

Is that why Drew's not going?

"Partially. I think he would be accepted as my friend, but until I see more for myself, I'd rather not risk it. It was a time of major social flux, and I'm not certain when the tide began to turn, so to speak."

"But you'll be safe."

"I'll be seen as a white male somewhere in his thirties. The United States in the nineteen sixties revolved around men who looked like me."

*

Dude, what is that? It's super ugly.

"The Embarcadero Freeway," Will replied. He didn't like it any more than I did. "It was functional but never completed. In twenty-four years it will sustain significant earthquake damage and will be demolished two years after that."

So, yay for the earthquake?

"People died in that earthquake, so no."

It was monstrously ugly, a vehicular thoroughfare that rose above the Embarcadero and cut off views of the bay. I couldn't understand why it had been built in the first place, but he assured me it'd had a purpose. Half of its purpose seemed to be pissing people off, but it relieved a traffic burden and connected the city. If not for the earthquake, it would have one day linked traffic from near the Bay Bridge all the way to the Golden Gate.

"People loved their cars," he said as we headed in the other direction, away from the Embarcadero. "It will be roughly another hundred twenty years before they seriously shift away from internal combustion engines. Between now and then the number of cars in use will quintuple."

It kinda stinks here.

The San Francisco of this When was crowded. Sidewalks were bursting with people rushing to get to their destinations, dodging curious tourists that kept blocking the way as they stopped to gawk at everything new to them. My nose stung with the aroma of the great unwashed masses comingled with the exhaust from the cars that rolled past, and I wondered how I had ever survived in this When.

Our destination was Ghirardelli Square, but Will wanted to get there by walking through downtown and then up Powell Street to Columbus, bypassing the Embarcadero. This route allowed him to feel the city's pulse; he could cross paths with a greater mixture of locals and tourists than he would by walking along what in our own When would be quieter and populated with more residents than visitors to the city.

I peeked out from my pocket in his jacket and was glad to have a safe space to hide. Will smelled like cherry soap and breathing in his scent was far better than what lingered in the air.

I poked my head back out when he paused on Union Square.

Did France invade San Francisco?

"What are you talking about, Wick?"

Over there. The Eifel Tower.

"Ah. No, that's just a sign on top of the building. In this When it's a department store called City of Paris. And home—" he pointed to a building across the street "—is right there."

That's home? It's broken.

"Not broken. It's merely different."

There's no balcony. It doesn't look right without a balcony. And it's not the same height all over.

"I expect many things will be different." He resumed the hike to Ghirardelli, marching up Powell Street as if the incline wasn't a big deal. We passed huffing, sweaty tourists, many who had stopped to catch their breath, and a few who uttered things from the Queen's bad word list when they realized their climb wasn't even halfway done.

"I saw a sidewalk with *stairs* built into it," one man complained as Will went past. "Effing stairs! Why didn't I stop to think that meant lots of hills?"

"We could have gone to New York," his companion said. "But no, you wanted to see the damned Golden Gate."

"I do, but the *hills*..."

To be fair, visitors to the city in our own When often had the same surprise. Pictures of San Francisco should have prepared them for the sight of long, sloping streets, but the reality was that walking through cities in Kansas or North Dakota didn't get anyone in shape for a stroll through San Francisco.

That's why we have cable cars, even hundreds of years later.

Well, that and cable cars are just cool.

While Will power-walked up Powell, I concentrated on not squirming and tried to look like a wallet. The next time I peeked out, we were near Washington Square, which oddly enough was not on Washington.

You shouldn't have cut your hair so short. Your old hair fits in just fine. Even the hair that pisses your mom off would have been fine.

"It would have been fine under other circumstances. We're about to go spy on a boy and may wish to converse with him. I need to look... safe."

Sheesh. White people.

"Just people, Wick. It's human nature to stereotype. We've simply evolved our stereotypes."

Fine. You all suck.

"Says the cat who harbors some specific notions about hippies."

You get kicked by one. See what you think then.

"You were really kicked? I admit, I assumed that was an exaggeration."

Like a rock across the street.

He paused again. "Wick, what did they do to you?"

It was a rhetorical question, words that were wrapped around sorrow and an apology for every horrible human that had ever existed in my world.

You can't change it, Will. No matter what you see, leave it alone. I did okay. I only want to know where I came from.

We came up the back side of Ghirardelli. Will wanted to get a good look at the aquatic park from a distance. He hadn't spent much time in this When—he had a vague memory of a few hours spent downtown in 1971, leaving before he had originally intended because of a protest against the Viet Nam war—so he had no idea what it would look like, if the park existed as expected outside of my jumbled memories or if there was just water lapping onto the sand, but if it had been built—if the bleachers as we knew them were there—there would be people.

There were people.

"It's in less than stellar condition," he said softly, loud enough for only me to hear. "I imagine this state of disrepair attracted some unsavory elements."

Hippies.

"Wick, I'm not certain that the people you had issue with were actual hippies. It seems to be counter-intuitive to their message of peace and love."

That was a front for rampant public bouncing and the consumption of skunky-smelling smoking suckers.

"Public sex?"

I've seen things, Will.

"Perhaps. Now I need to you to be quiet, all right? I'm going to head up to the main level and walk around the fountain to get an idea of the current layout."

I was quiet. That didn't mean I held still; there were things I wanted to see, things that might jog another memory or two. I took chances and peeked, even though half my field of vision was filled with the zipper on his jacket. He strolled; he was a tourist checking out a landmark, and there was nothing suspicious about that. After he'd circled the fountain, he sat on its edge and waited.

When there was no one close, I peeked again. *There were more people. Are we at the wrong day?*

"It's July third," he said. "I wanted to get a look around before the area becomes a mass of people waiting for the fireworks."

I might be here today.

"I know. I'm keeping an eye out."

You have two eyes. You should use both of them.

"Hush."

We were silent for the next half hour. He'd sat at the fountain long enough that lingering would have looked like stalking, and he still wanted to find the closest portal. One was located right around the corner, but in this When it could have been enclosed in a building or obstructed by a tree or sticking halfway out of a wall.

He could only hear it; he turned the corner and said it was there, but to what degree he wasn't sure. "Peek," he said. "Tell me what you see."

He held his jacket open a few inches, and I stuck my head out. The familiar misty pink entry was right where it should be, in a covered walkway, where someone moving through the upper level of Ghirardelli wouldn't notice if we used it.

Thinking of using it as an escape hatch?

"Possibly." He wanted it because he suspected we'd be popping back and forth a lot, looking for a small, scared cat and a boy I could only partially describe. Once he was satisfied that the portal was functional and accessible, he went down the stairs on the far side and crossed the street. He wanted to walk down to the aquatic park. There were more people near the water, and he thought he would get a better sense of this When if he could people-watch without suspicion.

I remember this. It's not the same in our When. But I was here a lot.

He flipped the front of his jacket open a bit more so that I could see better. We sat on the cement bleachers and watched swimmers in the cove and people lounging on blankets on the sand. No one sunbathed; it was a nice day, but a bit chilly, and Will thought it was a bit too unsettling for anyone to stretch out on the sand in a bathing suit and fully relax.

"I've been here in the late twentieth and early twenty-first centuries," he told me. "It will be a popular place for runners and swimmers, and often you'll find people sleeping on the beach and in the bleachers."

They sleep here now, too, mostly at night. There are homeless people in every When.

"I know. And unfortunately, in the next decade, the numbers here will rise significantly. As military members return from Viet Nam, far too many will be displaced and fall prey to a drug culture that will become incredibly pervasive."

Lots of drugs here, now.

"Yes, but largely cannabis. The skunky smoking suckers you spoke of. In five years or so, after the hippie movement you so loathe fades, the abuse of hard recreational drugs will become epidemic. You really did miss—"

Will, look.

He turned his head in the direction I was looking. There was a tall, older man in torn pants and a dirt-covered shirt sprinting across the beach, large rock in hand, yelling incoherently as he kicked sand up in all directions. Running desperately ahead of him was a tiny cat who had a tinier fish hanging from his mouth, and the old man screamed *Give it back!* at the top of his lungs. When he cocked his arm back, ready to launch the rock—which was at least as big as the cat—Will twitched.

You can't stop this. I was okay. Just wait.

He knew he couldn't interfere; this wasn't like fixing a mistake in the timeline, the way he had when six-year-old Oz drowned or when twelve-year-old Drew was murdered right in front of him. This wasn't like keeping sixteen-year-old Jax from being run over by a delivery van. Those were errors in time; this had happened, and I had survived, so he had to leave it alone no matter how hard it was to watch.

Still, he got to his feet. He couldn't stop himself. The only thing that kept him from shouting was the sound of sneakers on pavement, someone running hard and fast. The old man stopped in his tracks as a skinny teenager with flaming red hair darted toward him and scooped the cat up before he could be hurt.

"He's just hungry. Look at him, he's a baby! Leave him alone."

"So am I! It's mine!"

"You want the fish back?" The boy jerked it out of the cat's mouth and threw it at the old man's feet. "There's your stupid fish. It's only half a bite for you. It would have been a whole day's food for him."

Will patted me through his jacket: be quiet. Hide.

I ducked back in before the boy could see me.

"Might be all I get today, either, you little snot." I couldn't see, but the memory snapped into focus. He shoved the mangled, thumb-sized fish into the front pocket of pants that were stiff with sweat and grime and sand puffed up around his ankles as he stomped off.

Will sat back down. "That could have been ugly," he whispered.

There was a beat of quiet, and then, "Will!"

He twitched; without looking, I knew that Will was trying to cover any look of surprise. He forced himself to relax, and said easily, "Tad. Hello."

"I wondered if I would see you today. Every year like clockwork."

"Funny how that works out."

Tad chuckled. "Sometimes I think you show up just to say happy birthday."

"What other reason could there be?" Will laughed lightly. "Happy birthday. You're twenty-five now, right?"

"Fifteen," he snorted. "Same lame joke every year. Don't stop."

"How many years has it been?" Will asked.

There was a moment of quiet while Tad thought about it. "The first time I saw you was on my ninth birthday." He pointed toward the side of the bleachers closest to the Maritime Museum. "Over there."

"Indeed. Six years."

Tad scratched the top of the cat's head. "I get bigger, this little guy doesn't. But he's doing all right, I think."

"Presumably angry that he didn't get the fish. As one would be when losing their only meal of the day."

There were promises of food within a few minutes; Tad had a bologna sandwich at his mother's shop and would give the meaty bits to his furry friend and then let him loose near the park so he could hunt for something fresh.

He wasn't a great hunter, as evidenced by his size, but Tad occasionally found him tearing the meat out of a freshly killed bird and had once seen him destroy a rat that was nearly as big as he was, entrails and all.

I loathed the taste of rodent. I'd once caught a mouse in Aubrey and Jax's apartment but let it go after biting down because the taste was so foul. Now I wondered if it was truly all that repellant, or if I'd learned to hate it.

I hated killing. I didn't need my memories to know that.

"You know, sometimes I think he feels guilty about killing his own food. He takes down a rat, and it's like he sighs and apologizes to it before he rips it open. I've tried to tell him it's just the circle of life and all, but still. I get that vibe. He really hates it."

"Perhaps he's tired of his choices," Will said. "If he were bigger, he could take down a greater variety of game."

"Yeah, maybe. But I still think he'd feel bad about it. This cat has *soul*, Will."

"Indeed. I believe you're right."

Tad popped up. "Gotta go. Say goodbye to Will, Merlin. We'll see him next year."

I felt Will reach out to pet the cat's head. "I hope so."

Tad took a few steps. "Aw, man, maybe not. My mom is selling her shop. She wants to move to Sacramento. But if she doesn't get a buyer, I'll be here."

"Good luck to your mother," Will said. "And Sacramento is a decent place to be."

"Eh. Maybe. It gets too hot up there. Merlin can't go with us, and I don't know what will happen to him. Stupid allergies."

"I'll return to the area from time to time. I'll keep an eye out, and I may know someone who will come for him."

"Really? Thanks, Will!"

He patted his jacket when it was safe for me to peek out. "We have an obligation now, Wick. I hope nineteen-fifty-nine is not cold and rainy because we're apparently going to the beach."

5

It was not cold and rainy. It was hot, which made Will's jacket look out of place, but he couldn't take it off because I was lounging in the pocket. He couldn't pull me out and let me lounge nearby because I looked exactly like the other cat, and what if there was a mix-up? He didn't want any attention, other than from Tad, but everyone else was in t-shirts or lightly colored, short-sleeved button-down shirts, and no one else was wearing a jacket.

"Relax," he said as he sat down. "I'm from out of town. This feels cold to me, all right?"

Where would you be from that this *feels cold?*

"Las Vegas?"

It gets cold in Las Vegas at night. Doesn't it? You'd go outside a lot at night there.

"All right. Texas. Houston. It's hot and humid there."

Maybe you should be from Florida. You've been known to be that uptight.

"Stop. And Florida isn't a country in this When. It's merely a state to which old people flock during the winter."

Fine. You're from Texas. Yeehaw.
What's out there? Can I peek?

He thought I could safely take a quick look around. It hadn't changed in the ten minutes since we'd last been there six years from now, other than the people and the amount of sunlight. We were on the second step, not quite next to the Maritime Building. Will was sweating a bit, and I was caught up in the vortex of his body heat, and we were both uncomfortable.

There. Running along the bottom step.

I ducked back in as he turned. Little Tad, much shorter than he had just been, scrambled along the bottom step of the bleachers, his knees scraping concrete as a tired woman with hair as red as his trailed behind him.

"Leave the cat alone, Tad," she sighed. "You're scaring him."

"He likes me! I gave him the guts out of my sandwich yesterday."

I peeked. My other self was running on top of the step. He wasn't trying to get away, he was playing, and I whispered to Will, *I'm not afraid. I wanted to play with him. No one ever played with me, and it was my first real taste of fun.*

"Tad!"

Will sat up a bit straighter and laughed. The cat had launched at him and landed in his lap. He looked up at Will's face, then his chest, and hissed.

"I don't think your cat cares much for me," he told Tad.

Tad stopped several feet away, and the cat

jumped off Will's legs and happily went to him. "See, Mom? We're friends."

"Just keep him away from me." She sat on the first step, not far from Will. "I'm sorry if he bothered you. My son found the little guy near Ghirardelli a few days ago and has been worried sick about him. He's nothing but skin and bones. Tad can't stand the idea of that."

"Stray, then?"

"Probably. But with all the construction going on, he's convinced himself that the cat has been chased away from home and will die if he doesn't feed it."

Will turned in the direction of Ghirardelli Square, even though he couldn't really see it from here. "I'm not local. What construction?"

"They're turning the old factory into a tourist attraction. Shops and restaurants. Any critters living around it are probably unhappy right now." She laughed lightly. "I'm glad the only thing he found was a cat. At least I can argue against bringing that home. What if he'd found a puppy?"

"You don't like cats?" Will asked.

"No, I love them, but I'm allergic. This is as close as I dare get to him."

She couldn't let him bring the tiny cat home, but she agreed that he could come to the park every day to feed him. It pushed her out of the house and gave him something to look forward to. "He misses his daddy something fierce, even though I'm not sure he remembers him. This is the first time I've seen him so happy, not since before his daddy left for the war."

"He must have been very young," Will mused.

"Just three. The war was almost over, too, if he'd only come home a month earlier."

"I'm terribly sorry."

"Thank you. And listen to me, babbling on. I apologize."

I didn't have to see to know that Will smiled at her. "No apologies necessary. I can imagine it's been quite painful all these years. Raising a boy alone can't be easy."

"I have my momma and daddy helping. It's getting better." She laughed, the uneasy way people do when they need to change the subject. "Today is Tad's birthday, so we're going to think happy thoughts."

"Well, then." His voice got a bit louder as he called out, "Happy birthday, Tad."

"Thanks, mister." Small feet shuffled closer. "Hey, you want a cat? He needs a home."

"I wish I could," Will said. "But I already have a cat at home, and I don't think he would appreciate it if I brought home another. He's very old and very crotchety."

"He's super friendly. He would be nice to an old geezer cat."

Will chuckled and said, "He spit at me not five minutes ago."

"But he got in your lap. He was just playing."

"Ah. Still. I honestly would if I could, but it wouldn't be fair to my cat."

Tad sighed, hard. "All right. Come on, Merlin. You need to eat before I go home."

"Merlin," his mother said as she got up. "He showed up like magic. I just hope he doesn't vanish that way, too."

*

On Tad's tenth birthday he brought a can of tuna and sat near Will on the bleachers while Merlin ate. I could smell it from my spot inside Will's jacket and could feel the happiness on Merlin's tongue as if I were eating it myself. First, he would lap up all the water from the can, and then he would chew slowly, keeping the taste on his tongue as long as possible.

He'd learned that along the way. Tad could only come with food once a day, and it wasn't always as much as Merlin needed to thrive—Will realized then that Tad wasn't sure how much a small cat wanted to eat, and he often brought food not suitable for optimum feline health—so he tried to savor every bite when he was given something as wonderful as tuna.

"Does your cat like tuna?" Tad asked.

"Indeed, he does," Will said. "He likes shrimp more, but he's never turned his nose up at canned tuna. He drinks the water first, too."

"Yeah, my mom says that's probably because he's always thirsty. I think it's because he's saving the stinkiest part for last."

"Because it's his favorite, or because he's putting it off?"

"He loves it. I bet he'd love shrimp, too, but

my mom can't afford that, not even for herself, and I know she likes it. But you know what? When I grow up, I'm going to buy her shrimp for Sunday dinner every week. Shrimp and steak. Know what my grandpa calls that?"

Will knew but told Tad to enlighten him anyway.

"Surf and turf!" He cackled like it was the funniest thing he'd ever said. "Even when I have my own house, I'm going to hers for Sunday dinner, and that's what we're having."

"That sounds wonderful."

Tad sighed. "Once I get my own house, Merlin can live with me. He'll have a room of his own, and toys, and so much food he'll get super fat."

"Merlin's lucky to have you," Will told him, and not for the last time. "I look forward to seeing him fat and happy."

*

On Tad's eleventh birthday, there was ham. Will noticed that Merlin had a bit of a limp and pointed it out. Tad shrugged because there wasn't much he could do about it. "We get a lot of bums around here," he told Will. "Sometimes they throw things at him. Sometimes he gets kicked. You know, all Merlin does is try to sneak some of their food. I can't give him enough, and he's still not so great at hunting. But he's *super* brave and gets close to people so he can try to snatch something to eat."

"You've actually seen someone kick him?"

"Yeah. Mom saw it, too, and holy *smokes*, you should have seen her. She gave him what-for and promised if she saw it happen again, she was getting Mr. Cunningham to straighten him out."

"And that is?" Will prompted.

"Some guy she's dating. He's okay. Most everyone around here knows him. He's huge, you know, lots of muscles and nobody is gonna cross him."

Will wondered out loud what sort of person would physically attack an animal not much bigger than their own fist. Merlin was tiny; even if he pounced hard on someone, he wasn't hurting them. Surely anyone could see that he was hungry and only trying to feed himself.

I don't think he expected Tad to answer. It was a thought that whipped around his brain and then fell out of his mouth, but Tad had clearly considered it, too. "Some people don't stop to think that Merlin has real feelings. He's just a thing to them. Kicking him out of the way is the same thing as kicking a can off the sidewalk. They probably whack their own puppies on the nose for making mistakes, too. Like hitting ever does any good."

"Only in self-defense," Will mused.

"Yeah, maybe. I guess I would hit someone if they were picking on a girl, too. But you don't make someone learn by hitting them."

I felt Will lean back. "Has someone hit you?"

Tad snorted. "Nah. My grandpa spanked me once because I ran out into the street without looking, but he felt worse about that than I did. He said a good yelling would have gotten the point across, too. And my grandpa can yell."

"Mine as well," Will chuckled. "And yet, I think he was always right. He's still one of my favorite people."

"Wow. He's still alive?"

"Are you insinuating that I'm old?"

"Well, yeah. I mean, you gotta be thirty or something. That's at least halfway to dead."

*

On Tad's twelfth birthday, he mocked Will for never changing clothes. "Same pants, same jacket. You own other stuff, right?"

"I'm comfortable," Will asserted. "That's all that matters."

"How can you be comfortable? I'd be sweating bullets if I had to wear a jacket today. I mean, it's not hot, but it's not cold, either. People are swimming, for Pete's sake."

"This is a bit chilly for me," Will said. "What about you, do you ever get out there to swim?"

"Nah. Never learned how. Lessons are for snotty rich kids. You swim?"

"If I say yes, you'll toss me in with the rich kids you seem to dislike."

"Depends on who taught you, I guess."

Will wasn't about to tell him he learned to swim in an indoor pool housed five floors down from the apartment at home. He said he was taught by his father and mother, which was true, but he left out the lab's techs who also spent time making sure he knew how to not drown before he was even five years old. Nor that the house was once the home to the country's kings and queens.

"What's that like?" Tad asked. He sounded far away, like he'd gotten up to move down the bleachers. I strained to hear; he was picking Merlin up. A moment later he was sitting near Will again, and I could hear Merlin purring.

"Swimming?"

"Having a dad to teach you stuff. I don't remember mine."

"I don't think I fully appreciated him when I was a boy," Will said. "I was grown before I realized how comforting his presence was. Even now I find it necessary to remind myself that he's an incredible person, and I should spend more time with him."

"Yeah, really. Spend a lot of time with him. He's gotta be really old by now. Was he a good dad?"

"Very good."

Tad let out a heavy breath. "Yeah. Then you owe him."

Will was quiet for long enough that I wanted to peek out and see what was wrong. Then Tad's breath hiccupped, and I felt Will reach out, rubbing his hand across Tad's back. Softly, he asked, "What happened?"

"Grandpa died." His voice came out in a squeak. "I don't know what's gonna happen to us, Will. We needed him."

"I'm sorry," Will said, voice still soft.

With a giant sniff, Tad popped up. "Yeah, thanks. I gotta go. I'm okay. I swear."

*

Twenty minutes and a year later, Merlin was feasting on chicken, and Tad was several inches taller. He asked Will why he was there every year on his birthday, and never any other time.

"I'm only here for a day or two each year. One day I hope to stay. I'd like to live here."

"You got kids?"

"Not yet," Will answered, unsure why he'd suddenly asked. "Do you?"

That made Tad roar with laughter.

"Well, it is your birthday, and you're what now, twenty-five? It's possible."

"I'm thirteen. You're a dork."

"Ah, well, even so. I don't have children yet."

"Married?"

"I am. You?"

Tad snorted again. "My mom asked me, you know. She said that if I saw you again this year, I should look for a wedding ring."

Will held his hand up to show Tad his gold wedding band. "Why does she want to know? She met me once, years ago."

"She thought you were cute."

"I thought she was dating someone."

Tad had to think about it. "Oh, yeah. Cunningham. That was a long time ago, geez. She dumped him when he tried to forbid her from opening a store up there." He thumbed toward Ghirardelli. "Grandpa left her some money, and he wanted her to use it to go into business, so she did."

"Really now. That's wonderful."

"You think so? Yeah, she won't be happy to hear you're married."

"And I'm sorry about your grandfather. How are you and your mother holding up?"

"I'm okay, but she misses him a lot. For a year it's just been my mom and me and my grandma, but I think Grandma's going to move to Kentucky to live with my aunt and uncle. They have a huge house and a bunch of kids. She thinks they need her there."

"I'm sure you'll miss her." Will leaned back, his elbows on the bleacher step behind us. "I know when my grandparents moved to Scotland, it took a long time before I stopped missing them so much. Truthfully, I always do, but it did get better after some time."

"Huh, are they Scottish? I guess that explains why you have that accent sometimes."

Will acknowledged the accent and blamed his mother for it. "She has a significant burr, and years of listening to her rubbed off on me."

"But you're an American, right?"

"Born right here in San Francisco," he said. "It's why I keep coming back. This is home."

"You here for vacation or work stuff?"

"Work," he said. "I've needed to return every year to take care of a few things for a very pushy and vocal boss. But I don't mind, really."

"My mom's a pushy boss," Tad said, laughing. "I work a couple hours after school every day, stocking shelves and stuff. And she actually makes me work!"

Will laughed right along with him. "Imagine that. Having to earn your paycheck."

"Paycheck. I don't get paid. I do it because she needs someone. That's what men do, right?"

"Indeed."

"Grandpa always said he wanted me to be a good man. He said that good men do the right thing, treat women like ladies, work hard, and then life will treat them good right back. Think he was right?"

"I do. I've told my younger family members more than once to decide the kind of man they want to be, and then be it. It truly is up to you."

"Well, I wanna be like my grandpa. He took care of people. He even liked that I take care of Merlin. 'Don't ever stop doing things like that,' he said. So I won't."

"I think I would have liked your grandfather," Will told him.

I heard Tad get up, and his feet slide on the cement bleacher. "Yeah, you would have. Never met anyone who didn't."

I'm telling Aisha you were flirting with a strange woman.

"I did not," he said as we headed for the portal. "I had a very short conversation with her, and it was years ago."

Couple hours ago.

"For me."

Totally flirted with her.

"One more birthday," Will sighed. "Let's get this done, and then we can move on."

*

We waited in the bleachers for two hours. It was cold and foggy, which made Will wonder if Tad would show up. He might have been there earlier; he might come later. We knew he would come, though, because when he was fifteen, he told Will that he was there every year. That had to mean he'd been there on his fourteenth, and Will had spoken with him.

He'd made sure I'd peed before we got there, so I curled up in the pocket of his jacket to take a nap. He might have been chilly, but I had his body heat wrapped around me, and sleeping would have been a very easy thing to do. I had nearly drifted off when Will's weight shifted, and I heard tiny paws coming toward him.

"Well, hello," Will said. "Where's Tad?"

'Soon. Here soon. You're in the wrong time.'

Will leaned forward, but he didn't say anything.

'I smell me. On you. I smell old.'

I wanted to peek out, but I also didn't want to freak myself out.

'I hear me. Let me see. Look.'

Will patted his chest, inviting me to poke my head out.

'Your person hears me?'

He hears you, but I don't know if he understands you.

"I understand him. Merlin, do you mind if we ask you a few questions?"

'Okay.'

"Do you know how you got here? Or how long you've been here?"

'As long as long is. There were stars. Forever.'

How long is forever, dude? Who took care of you before Tad?

'Forever is forever. The before time is hazy. There were stars.'

But you know you're me, right?

'You are me. Ancient.'

"What's the oldest thing you remember, Merlin?"

He sat on the bleacher and took his time to consider the question. *'The world fell apart. It rattled, and then things broke and burned, and people cried.'*

"Earthquake," Will mused.

How many people ago was that? How many fed you between then and now?

'None in my thinks.'

Dude, we're trying to figure out where you started.

'In the stars. I started in the stars.'

You're not an alien from outer space.

'There was nothing. Then there were stars. Then there was rain.'

How long was it between that and the earthquake?

'Three sunshines, no more.'

"Was the aquatic park here?" Will asked, gesturing to the semi-closed bay.

'Yes. But different.'

I want to ask what life was like, but I don't think I would have understood when I was him.

Dude, can you read? Do you ever get any news?

'Some words. I hear radio. See TV in windows.'

"Was there TV when you started in the stars?"

'No. People talked. I listened.'

What's the oldest news you remember?

'The world was broken and burning.'

I don't know how to ask him anything else, Will. I feel like I should know what he's talking about.

Will went in another direction. "Do you know who Roosevelt was?"

'Which? There were two.'

He patted his chest again, so I ducked back in and listened to the sound of Tad approaching. He was laughing; he'd seen Will talking to Merlin.

"That looked like a real conversation."

"I have been known to talk to cats for longer than seems appropriate," Will said. "Happy birthday. Twenty-five, right?"

"Fourteen," he snorted. "So, what were you and Merlin talking about?"

"Food, I imagine. He seems hungry."

"Are you?" Tad asked Merlin. "I have a chunk of roast beef that Mom cut up and some smelly dry cat food."

'Dry food.' Merlin exhaled sharply, an exasperated huff that didn't go unnoticed.

"You're awfully picky for someone who doesn't get to eat much," Tad said as he peeled open the foil pouch he'd brought with him. "He hates the dry food, but my mom says it's probably better for him than leftovers. Our neighbor lets me take what her cat doesn't eat in the morning."

"Does Merlin eat it?" Will asked.

"Yeah, but I get the feeling he's cussing at me every time I give it to him."

"Let him cuss. He's lucky you feed him."

'I know that.'

Tad snorted. "He nicked some fried fish from a guy sitting on a bench the other day. Just jumped up, grabbed it right out of his hand, and ran. The guy he stole from started laughing because he couldn't believe that tiny thing was so brave, but this...idiot...threw a shoe at Merlin. It wasn't even *his* fish. Hit him right upside the head, too."

"He was all right?"

"Yeah. Knocked him over, but he got right back up, hissed at the guy, and then wolfed the fish down. And while he was eating, I got to watch two grown men get into a fist fight because one was mad that a cat had nicked someone else's lunch, and the other thought it was funny, and it was *his* lunch. They *punched* each other over it."

'People are apes.'

"Righteous indignation," Will said. "People always have and always will allow their tempers to get the better of them in situations where their opinions should not matter."

"No kidding." He set down the packet with the

dry food. "Come on, Merlin, don't make a liar out of me."

"Perhaps remove it from the foil," Will said. "It may hurt a bit when his teeth touch it."

"What, like feed him on the ground?"

"On the bleacher step. He eats off the ground when you're not looking. It's fine."

'I lick my own butt, too. He's right, it's fine.'

"Geez, don't tell my mom if you see her. She thinks it's undignified to make him eat with dirt on his food."

"She's quite kind, isn't she?"

"She's all right." He laughed abruptly. "I told her you were married. I think a week later she started dating this other guy. I mean, I know it was a coincidence, but it was funny anyway."

"Good for her."

"He moved here from Denver. He's this thing she digs." He thought about it for a moment. "A feminist. That's a guy who thinks women are just as good as men."

"Indeed. I feel the same way."

"Well, yeah, they're good and all, but I dunno. You think it's okay for a woman to just do whatever she wants, no matter what her husband thinks?"

"That's not feminism, Tad. Feminism is about equality, and I do believe that women are equal to men. Both people in a relationship should have an equal say in the matters of their lives."

"Huh. Well, he thinks women should get paid the same as men, too. Like they—"

"They should."

"But men have families to raise!"

"Consider this," Will said carefully. "You're a single man working as, say, a ninth-grade teacher. In the next classroom is a war widow who has three children, and she teaches the same subject that you do, to the same number of students. By your logic, should she be paid more?"

"No. He should. He's the—"

"Man? But she has a family to raise, children to feed and clothe, whereas he does not."

"Maybe."

"Your argument was predicated on a man having a family to raise. In this scenario, he has no family, and she does. So, who then should logically draw the larger paycheck? Or perhaps the pay should be based on the work itself, and not the number of mouths at home in need of being fed?"

Tad grunted. "It just doesn't seem right."

Will decided to poke the bear. "Your mother has been raising you alone for eleven years. Do you honestly think she hasn't worked just as hard as the men around her? She's been a mother, opened her own business, and as far as I can see has done well. Doesn't that count for something?"

"My mom's not a wo—"

'And the penny drops.'

"Oh. Wow. She is a woman, I guess."

"Indeed." Will sounded amused, but he didn't laugh.

"What about you? Do you let your wife work?"

"My wife doesn't need permission from me to do anything, Tad. She teaches advanced math at a college level. She's smarter than I am, works just as hard if not harder, and deserves more than she gets for the effort she gives."

"Yeah, but I bet you don't want her to make more than you do."

"I would be quite content if she did."

"Other people would talk about—"

"The opinions of others are irrelevant. No one else gets a say in my marriage. If people are wont to gossip because my wife draws the larger pay and are scandalized by it, that's not my problem. It's theirs."

"You know, you don't look anything like the feminists I've met. I would have pegged you for someone like my grandpa, before he died. He always said that women belonged at home, keeping house and raising babies, and it was up to good men to make sure they were happy."

"And yet, he left your mother the funds to open her own shop."

"Huh. Wow. He did, didn't he?" There was another beat of quiet. "Does it bug you that your wife is smarter?"

"Not at all. I appreciate that she can challenge me. Her strengths bolster my weaknesses. I believe it makes me a better man."

"Huh. Yeah, maybe." He got up. "Gotta get going. Dale—that's her boyfriend—is taking us out to dinner for my birthday."

"I hope it's quite enjoyable," Will said. "Do you like him?"

"Yeah, he's a nice guy. Maybe nicer than I thought."

Why do you care if he's a nice guy?

"I believe I'm starting to care about that boy's life," Will admitted.

Merlin finished the last bite of kibble and started to walk away until Will called to him. "If I tell you something, will you remember it a year from now?"

'I will.'

"We'll be here on his next birthday. He'll take you with him to get food when he leaves. After he's fed you, come back. We'll return as well."

'I'll remember.'

*

Will made sure we wouldn't run into ourselves. We rounded the far side of the Maritime Museum as the earlier versions of us departed on the other side, heading for the portal, and he sat away from the spot where we'd first met Tad.

"Merlin," Will said, "does not have a transponder. Yet I understood him perfectly. I think that safely eliminates that as the reason you and I are able to converse."

You don't know if he has one or not, not yet.

"You didn't come home with one, you know. Dad implanted two in you, after you'd been with us for some time. It stands to reason that he checked before doing that."

Maybe our lives are all one big simulation, and the computer did it anyway.

He didn't dismiss the idea, and I was spared a lecture on theories that the universe was one big simulation when Merlin hopped up onto the bleacher.

'I remembered. I came back.'

"Thank you," Will said. "It's important."

'Let me see me.'

I stuck my head out. *Here you are.*

"Merlin, you know Tad is moving away?"

'To Sacramento. His mother is marrying the feminist and closing her shop to stay home and have babies. Ironic.'

"Regardless. He can't take you with him."

'Her allergies. I know.'

That's a bogus reason. You could go and live outside there the same as here.

"We're not judging, Wick. That's not why I wanted to speak to him."

'I'm judging. It's mean. The feminist should be nicer and allow me to come. But I'll be fine.'

"I won't promise you'll be fine. You'll survive, but it's going to be very hard on you. Tad protects you more than you realize, I think. The next year will be physically and emotionally demanding for you in ways I cannot fathom."

'So was the before time.'

"One year from now, actually eleven months, you need to be in the Haight. Do you know where that is?"

'Hippies. Yes.'

"Look for a man who looks a little bit like me." Will gave him a detailed description of Finn, where and when they would meet. "Ask him for food. Beg him. Loudly. He won't understand the words, but after a minute or two he'll understand that you're hungry and he'll feed you. While he's feeding you from his sandwich, he'll offer to take you with him. Let him pick you up. He'll bring you home where you'll live with his family. He has a little boy who will love—"

'He'll take me home to you.'

"Indeed. I am that little boy."

None of this surprises you, does it?

'I came from the nothing and the stars. Anything is possible. Except for cheese. I don't think that's possible anymore. I miss cheese.'

"Finn's sandwich will have cheese in it," Will promised him. "Beef and cheese, and I swear to god, I'll spend the rest of my life stuffing you with it."

6

He needed to go home, even if it was just for a night. I felt cramped stuck in that pocket with my tail tucked between my legs and no way to really stretch, so there was no argument from me. We went back to the portal near the Plaza and popped out a few minutes after we'd left, and he went straight to the coffee shop where Aisha waited with Aubrey.

"That was quick," Aisha said, even though she knew it wasn't. "Did you find Wick's friend?"

He did, and he promised to stuff him with cheese. Where's my cheese?

"Please tell me you have cheese," he said as he bent over to give her a quick kiss. "Cheese or bacon, he'll be happy with either."

"Yes, sweetie, I have half a pound of gouda in one pocket and a half a pound of sliced smoked bacon in another."

"No need to get sarcastic." He set me on a chair, told me to sit tight, and that he would be right back.

I love guilt.

What are we talking about?

Aisha rubbed the top of my head and went right back to her conversation with Aubrey, which seemed to be mostly grumbling about teaching and overprotective parents, and one unfortunate father who'd forgotten that his little snowflake's teacher was also the Queen. He was five kinds of upset that his little girl had been denied recess and threatened with additional punishments; he stormed into the classroom yelling things that were right smack in the middle of the Bad Word List, which caused two of her guards to pop out of their hiding places.

She made them wait at the back of the classroom while she assured him that she was not, as his daughter swore, super mean and really, really unfair. "She'd cheated on a math test, kicked another student, and then topped it all off by stealing someone's lunch from their backpack. All before noon. She's lucky that having recess withheld was her only punishment."

"She stole someone's lunch? That's a suspension-worthy offense. Well, so's the kicking."

"Like I said, she was lucky."

"New behavior?"

"New enough that I'm keeping an eye on her."

Will set a plate with a small mound of chopped up bacon on the table in front of me. "No cheese, I'm sorry."

This is acceptable.

"I thought it might be." He kissed Aisha again, gave Aubrey a quick one on her cheek, and took the last chair at the table. "What did I interrupt?"

"Whining," Aubrey said. "And I've gotten it out of my system. Tell us about your trip."

He told them about bouncing from birthday to birthday, conveniently leaving out the part where he flirted with Tad's mom and the day she wanted to know if Will was married. By the time he finished, explaining how he had told Merlin where to find Finn and how insistent he needed to be, Aubrey was crying, and Aisha reached across the table for me.

Will pulled me out of her hands and set me back on the chair. "At least let him finish eating before you manhandle him. There's still a microscopic layer of bacon grease he hasn't licked up."

Thank you. And that was sexist. She'd be ladyhandling me. When there's no bacon, I enjoy that.

"Wick was starving when Tad found him. He'd managed to keep himself alive, but I don't think he was anywhere close to thriving."

"Perhaps that explains his size," Aubrey said.

"It might. But he'd been alive for a very long time by then, long past his formative years."

"What did he remember?" Aisha asked.

"The earthquake of nineteen-hundred-six," Will said. "And it's a long shot, but I want to go and try to find him then. If he's there, he might have a better idea of where he came from."

*

He needed different clothes. Again, Mrs. Kovlov didn't ask why, but she admitted to a bit of excitement over creating something straight out of a history book. He'd asked that the clothes not look new, and she assured him that they would be worn and comfortable, and she would have another special pocket just for me.

His plans put us in 1906 San Francisco during a time of day when he doubted we'd even be seen, but he went through the trouble of dressing the part, just in case. He typically visited Whens where his usual clothing fit in, and he took care to not stand out; this was the furthest back he'd ever gone, and he wasn't sure what he should expect.

Finn wasn't sure how far back the portals would be reliable. Theoretically, Will should be able to step through to any time that had ever existed between Finn's oldest date lived and the beginning of everything, but Finn wasn't going to swear to it. And even if the portals worked Whenever, there was no guarantee they were accessible. The portal with clear access in 2417 might have a giant boulder wrapped around it in 1517. He'd only made sure of accessibility for the periods of time he intended to take people fleeing from the end of everything.

It was worth the chance. He didn't voice the notion that we could become stuck halfway through if the destination were blocked off. He pointedly didn't remind anyone what had happened when he tried to step through from 2415 to a future that had ended. We were in the portal, able to move a bit but not turn around, and if not for Oz, he and I might still be stuck there.

"I'm not happy about this," Aisha told him the night before we left, snuggled next to him in bed. "I pulled up information about that earthquake while you were getting your suit fit. It destroyed—"

"I won't be there when the earthquake hits," he promised. "We're heading for two days prior, and we won't stay long enough to be caught up in any foreshocks."

"You better not, mister."

"The first shock was felt at approximately five-twelve in the morning, April eighteenth. We'll arrive before dawn on the sixteenth, and I don't think we'll stay a full day."

I won't let him stay. If he tries, I'll pee on him, and then he'll have to come home and change clothes.

Aisha patted the mattress and asked me to come over and sleep with them. She declared that it was too cold by the window—it wasn't—and if we were going away again in the morning, she wanted us both in bed with her all night.

I don't want to get in your way.

"Wick," Will sighed. "Half the reason we bought a bed this insanely big was to give you space to sleep with us. And you're never in the way."

I enjoyed my spot on the window seat but wasn't going to upset Aisha. And their bed was massive, big enough for them, Jay, and three of their friends if they didn't mind being pressed up against each other…something I hoped I'd never witness. While she continued to fuss over Will, I moved to the foot of their bed.

"We'll be gone for all of an hour, at most," Will reminded her. "Less than five minutes, realistically."

She reached for his wrist and set his hand on her stomach. "I don't care. Right now, it feels like you're leaving for a long time. And if something happens…"

"I will do nothing to put either of us at risk." He moved his hand and placed a long, gentle kiss on the spot where it had been. "I won't miss any of this. I swear."

All of this can wait until after the baby is born. The past isn't going anywhere.

"I know it could, Wick, but I sense you need me to do this now. You're worried you'll forget, and I know how much that matters to you."

I curled up near his feet. *Can you take some cheese with us?*

"You'll survive an hour or two without eating."

Not for me. For him.

"Will that matter to the timeline?" Aisha asked.

It didn't matter.

He was taking some cheese.

*

It was dark on the other side of the portal. Will wanted to arrive before dawn, reasoning that there wouldn't be many people at or around Union Square before sunrise. His sudden presence might surprise one or two people who would blink, look again, and brush it off to either needing more sleep or fewer sips from their flask. He stepped out and shivered, pulling his coat a little tighter, though it didn't feel especially cold to me.

I poked my head out. Nothing looked right. The statue was where I expected it, but the buildings that surrounded Union Square were wrong, and the streets felt unfinished. The Square wasn't raised from the street level and there was wet grass where there I expected concrete; it could have been a park. It might have been a park. Finn's lab would not fit under this Union Square. There was no light bleeding from the structures surrounding us, and quiet crackled like wispy static that made the tiny hairs on my ears twitch.

"In two days, everything around here will be either destroyed or gutted. Union Square will become a campground for survivors."

Is that what made you shiver?

"Indeed. I am haunted by an event yet to happen and knowing I can do nothing about it invokes a peculiar sense of impotence."

I'm sorry.

We can't make a difference for the people right now. But maybe we can make a tiny difference for a cat. You remembered the cheese?

He patted his front pocket. "I have the cheese. And a bit of ham."

Then let's go find me. I hope I remember where I'm from.

He turned in the direction of Ghirardelli Square, walking fast enough that I bounced off his chest. "Wick, whatever you do, don't tell him he'll still be wandering around here in sixty years. We don't know what your frame of mind was then. It might terrify him."

Tell me about it.

"Are you remembering?"

A little bit. I remember meeting the happy birthday man and smelling me on him. I was happy that he could talk to me and didn't understand why no one else could.

"Was telling you about Finn a mistake?"

I'm not sure I would have been there when he was if you hadn't. I would have stayed near the aquatic park and starved to death, I think. If Finn hadn't found me, I think I would have died soon.

I know Will wondered: did I remember him because I'd just revisited that time and created a false memory, or had it triggered something inside my head?

My brain told me I was looking at him from Merlin's point of view. He sat on the bleachers with his feet perched on the cement in front, talking to himself as I walked across that first bleacher seat. He'd brightened when he noticed me, and he'd said hello.

That was a memory, not a wish.

Will? Stop for a minute?

He slowed and then stopped, pulling his jacket open to see me. "Problem?"

I remember you from then.

"And that tells me we're on the right track."

But we died. This is the first loop of time that we lived. You and I didn't go back before, we never went to see me. How we were there? I mean, how can I remember you if the last one of you died before we could do this?

"You're certain what you envision is a memory?"

I know it is.

He started walking again, but slower. "Finn's theories about time are simply that. Theories. He thinks of time as linear, and as our timeline progresses, it erases the things in front of us."

Like, how old Oz and Drew's past hasn't changed, even though it has for us?

"Indeed. Their Emperor and Wick died, and yet we can still go visit them, despite having lived past the days our other selves perished. The fact that we lived didn't change their past. And yet, I've made changes that took hold. I've manipulated my past to benefit my now."

You opened bank accounts and invested money.

"And those things took hold, as well. I clearly remember the pain of Oz drowning when she was six, and I remember changing that, yet her death is also not part of my timeline. Perhaps it only matters that we are here now, we would have gone back, and what you remember are echoes of events that *should* have occurred."

What you mean is that you have no idea.

"Clearly."

I knew he didn't like to examine the details of what happened when he changed things in the timeline; he interfered when things happened he was certain should not have, and his changes stuck. But he had no explanation for why I remembered the happy birthday man because our deaths in the last loop of time should have meant we were never there.

That didn't stop me from poking the bear, asking question after question, until we were almost to Ghirardelli Square. When we were less than half a mile away, we both fell silent, listening for the ghosts around us, the ghosts yet to come. He patted me through the fabric of his jacket, trying to reassure and comfort me, but what I felt was a crushing sadness and the terror of being utterly, completely alone.

*

The chocolate factory buildings were not identical to the Ghirardelli Square in our When, so Will didn't presume he would be able to find the portal. He knew that if it was not enclosed in a place we had no access to, then it was likely to be blocked by trees, the entry too obstructed to gain access. He counted on nothing being familiar; he hadn't had enough time to study the particulars of the area around Ghirardelli Square in early twentieth century San Francisco and didn't know how much of the chocolate factory was standing, nor which parts of it were operational.

"I do know this was all part of Black Point," he said as we made our way past Fort Mason. "And swimmers enjoy the cove, which essentially is our aquatic park. There's a rather large pipe that runs through it, discharging warm water from the factory's cooling system. It creates a pleasant area for swimming, even when the water on the edges of the park are too cold."

Okay.

Is there going to be a test on this? I'll take notes.

"Fine. I was simply sharing."

Go ahead. Share.

He huffed, and his breath turned to fog. "For someone who requested I do this, your sarcasm is unnecessary."

You could have said no.

He stopped. We were close to the chocolate factory, not far from the spot where he doubted he would find the portal. "No, Wick, I could not have denied you this. You have a right to your history and access to your memories."

What if my memories suck?

"You have a right to know that, as well."

Get moving then. If this sucks I want it over with fast.

"Are you cold?" he asked as he resumed his fast pace.

I'm stealing your warms. I'm fine.

Still, he covered me with his hand from outside his coat, and after a minute I felt the heat leach through. Until then, I hadn't realized that I was a bit chilly and I was grateful that he kept it there until we were on the other side of the factory. When he scrambled up a small slope, looking for the portal, his hand dropped away.

"I'm sorry, Wick. I need you to look. Does any of this seem familiar?"

I poked my head out; we were in a snarl of trees, standing next to a brick wall. The portal was behind it. Will lamented that, because if the portal was there, so might be my younger self, but there was a feeling of familiarity under the trees, and I was certain I'd been there before.

A bitter, foul taste filled my mouth.

There are rats here. Fat, slow rats.

Take me out.

He slipped me out of his coat, and I sat in the crook of his arm where I could press against his chest for warmth. The trees were thick, with branches that twisted and knotted against each other; soft, new leaves had sprouted near the tops, but the lower canopy was uncomfortably bare. It was quiet, except for the gentle sound of water dripping nearby.

There are birds living in the trees.

"As birds do."

These birds are mean. They'll peck at your head and then steal food right out of your mouth. If you don't have food, they'll dive at you and peck at your ears just because they can. And their feet are pointy and sharp, and they'll try to grab you from behind.

"Ah. That explains a lot."

The dripping became louder, and water pinged off my ears.

Rain.

"Not rain," Will said. "This is simply fog accumulated on the leaves. Aisha checked the weather before we left. It didn't rain on this day in nineteen-hundred-six."

It feels like rain.

"There's a reason for that, you know."

What was that you said about sarcasm?

He chuckled and told me to take a closer look. He had no idea in which direction we should go, nor how far from the factory a tiny me would have explored. As the dripping from the leaves increased, he cupped his hand over my head, trying to keep me dry, but he didn't force me back into his coat and waited patiently as I absorbed the surroundings.

Food was near here. I don't think I ventured far for a while. But I also don't know if a while was a day or two or year or two. But I was new when I was here. I think I stayed close.

That was good enough for him. We made our way between the trees, scanning the ground and the lower tree branches for signs of a small, frightened cat. Will paused frequently, intentionally quiet, and we listened as carefully as we looked.

Here. Stop here.

We'd looped back toward the factory wall, and a tiny voice in the back of my head told me that we needed to stop and wait right there. Will sat on the wet ground and tucked me inside the jacket, but not in the pocket, and let me watch with him. We needed to be patient because I was nearby and scared, and if he moved too fast or spoke loudly, he'd scare me away.

"This could take a while," Will whispered. "Tell me if you get too cold."

I didn't think it would be long before we spotted me. I had a vague feeling tickling the back of my brain, something that wasn't quite a memory so much as it was an awareness that I'd been here and terrified, and then had found something that calmed me. Hiding in the trees had been safe, safer than venturing out where there were people and noises that I couldn't make sense of. I'd been cold and wet, and even though I was now stealing Will's warms, I fought a shiver that wanted to snake its way up my spine.

That would only make him worry. I steeled myself against it and waited.

I'm out here somewhere. I'm close, I'm sure of it.

"It's not even dawn yet. You might be sleeping right now," he said, keeping his voice soft. "Is any of this jogging your memory?"

I looked up, peering through a spot where tree branches parted, leaving a view of the sky. I had a sensation of falling, stars flying past my face, and I was afraid but had no idea what of. I told Will that; I was too new to be wary of what I was feeling, not until I realized I was alone in this place. That feeling was overwhelming, and I'd had no idea what to do.

Maybe I climbed a tree and fell out. I got up there, saw the stars, and then fell.

"But we still need to know how you got here."

I might have been born here. I was new, I'm sure of it.

"Possibly."

Quiet now.

My gut told me we needed to stop talking. It sounded like an order when I told him to be quiet, but he didn't bristle against it. He stopped talking and peered into the darkness, taking care to not even breathe too loud.

I spotted me first, peeking around the trunk of a tree just five feet away. I saw an ear and one eye, twitching whiskers, and nudged Will so that he would see me, too.

He resisted the urge to call out, and he forced himself to not move.

I pushed my way out of his coat and sat on the ground near his feet, waiting for one ear to become two, and for whiskers to stop twitching in fear and begin quivering with hope. He finally stepped out from behind the tree and watched me, and then looked at Will. There was fear glimmering in his eyes, but along with that was longing, and I know Will saw it.

Come on, little dude. We won't hurt you.

He cocked his head.

We can help.

His head tilted back as he sniffed the air.

You know me. You can smell me, I smell just like you do.

One paw went to his face. He licked it, then sniffed it, and sniffed the air again.

I promise we won't hurt you.

He took three deliberate, cautious steps toward us, and then paused to sniff the air again. He knew my scent; it was Will he was focused on, trying to decide if the giant human was safe to approach.

It took half an hour and inch-long baby steps for him to get close enough to touch. Will knew better; he let the cat come to me first, and then waited. I sat still as he touched his nose to mine, and then as he sniffed my lips and my whiskers, and I let him lick my ears. When he was sure I was not a threat, he started sniffing Will's feet and worked his way up his leg.

When he reached Will's front pocket, he began pawing at it, first in hope and then frantically, and he finally let out a tiny, squeaky, 'meow.'

The man's hand is going to move. He won't hurt you.

Will slowly reached into his pocket for the cheese and the ham, and when he started to unfold the cloth around it, little me danced in excitement, shuffling from one foot to the other. He was fed in tiny bites; Will didn't want to give him too much at once, and I told him several times to slow down. There was more, but we didn't want him to throw up.

When he'd eaten half, he sat back and finally looked Will in the eyes.

The human's name is Will. He's going to talk now, all right? He'll try to not be loud.

"Hello," Will said softly. "Do you have a name?"

'Meow.'

Will sighed, disappointed.

Think in English, little dude.

'Meow?'

People-speak. Think the way people speak. Use their words, and he'll understand.

'Seven.'

"Your name is Seven?"

'Call me.'

People called him Seven, Will.

"How old are you, Seven? Do you know?"

'Old?'

How long have you been alive? Do you know how many days?

'All.'

"Of course. You've been alive for all of your days, haven't you?"

Where did you come from, Seven? I don't think you're from this When. Do you know? Where you're from?

'Stars.'

"Merlin said the same thing," Will said.

He's not an alien.

"I realize that. But it's a clue, nevertheless."

How did you get here from the stars? I asked Seven. Can you show us?

He turned and ran into the trees. I took off after him, counting on Will to keep up. Seven wound his way back and forth, seemingly without direction, and he did it with such abandon that I was afraid he was playing instead of leading us anywhere.

On his third circle of a single tree, I realized he was giving Will a chance to catch up, and the thing he wanted us to see was in the center of the circle he'd taken me around. Once Will was there, Seven darted to the middle and sat down, waiting for Will to see.

He crouched in the dirt. There were chunks of white metal, sheared by stress, scattered in a wide swath. Will dug a few of them from the dirt and turned each over in his hand, and on the third one he sat down, hard.

Attached to the backside of the largest piece was a coil-wound cable, and fused to its other end was a tiny, egg-shaped pod.

"A solar battery," he whispered.

He gathered as many pieces as he could find and set them in a pile. There was no mistaking it; they were slivers of one of Finn's egg-shaped time machines, fractured beyond any hope of repair.

*

I sat on Will's shoulder as Seven ate a little more of the cheese and the few bits of ham. He was sitting on the ground, leaning against the brick wall, and barely blinked as he watched Seven chew.

"He's so small," Will whispered.

I know what you're thinking. We can't take him with us, not even just long enough to make sure he's not hurt in the earthquake.

"Perhaps we're meant to. This city was brought to its knees, Wick. He may have survived because we took him through a portal, and then brought him back."

You know better.

"No, I really don't."

Will, the closest portal you can get to is probably on Market Street. We didn't take him all that way, go through, turn around to come back onto a street that was probably filled with smoking rubble and screaming people, and then bring him back here. You know we didn't do that.

"But look at him."

He's the same size I am, maybe half a pound lighter.

"He's at least a pound and a half lighter. And look at the way he's eating. He's starving."

No, he's tasting cheese for the first time. He's eating like that because this is the closest to bouncing he'll ever get. His mouth is really, really happy right now.

"What would it hurt, Wick?"

You'd be changing my history when it doesn't need to be changed. Look at me.

He continued to watch Seven eat.

Really, Will, look at me. See me in him.

With a sigh, he turned his head. "I know, you're fine. You survived. But I feel responsible for him, and I want—"

Don't change my life, Will.

Very softly, he said, "This is breaking my heart."

He'll be okay. I promise.

Seven licked up the last of the ham and

looked up at Will; he could smell the last few bites of cheese Will had in his hand, and he wanted it, but I'd asked Will to save it for the end, to make it easier to go.

Don't worry. You get a few more bites, but you need to listen to me first, all right?

'Yes.'

In two more days, two more sunshines, the world is going to get very loud, and it's going to break into pieces. There's going to be fire and people shouting, and you won't be sure what to do.

"Wick," Will breathed out.

It's scary, you're going to be scared. But you need to stay here, by this building and these trees, all right?

'Yes.'

You're going to be very hungry basically all the time, and most people aren't like Will. They won't give you food. They're going to yell at you and chase you away. If you get close to food, snatch it up and run away with it, okay? It's the only thing stealing is okay for. Do you understand? You're allowed to steal food. You have to steal food.

'Yes.'

People will also throw away food they don't want into big containers called trash cans. Don't climb in them, okay? You'll get stuck.

'Yes.'

Tell me what I just said. I need to know you understand.

'Loud. World break. Fire. People yell. Take food. No trash.'

You're going to have to hunt. That means you'll have to kill other animals for food.

'No.'

You have to, Seven. You have to stay alive. Hunt and eat when you can, and don't let the birds scare you too much.

'Birds mean.'

Yeah, they are. If you can catch one, you can eat that, too. Other animals are safe to eat, remember that. If it's not an animal, sniff it carefully first to make sure it's food.

'Yes.'

Practice thinking in people words, too. You're going to see us again someday, and it will help if you remember how, okay?

'Yes.'

I asked Will to give him the last bits of cheese and told Seven that while he finished it, we were going to leave. I wanted him to remember everything, and if he did, he would be fine.

Stay near here until the world stops shaking, and you'll be all right.

'Yes.'

You're a good boy, Seven. Remember that, too.

7

Aisha waited for us on Union Square. He hadn't asked her to; in fact, we'd left home alone right after Will promised he would be back soon. We stood near the apartment's front door at nine in the morning, and he waited patiently as she held on to him longer than she usually did, then he kissed her slowly, sweetly, and swore we'd be back before she finished reading the morning news.

She followed a few minutes later and watched as we disappeared into the portal, and then waited on a bench nearby. After all, no matter how long we were there, if everything went all right we would return in the time it took to blink a dozen times. She wanted to be there when we came back because her heart told her it was going to be hard.

Her heart was right.

Part of him expected her to be there because he barely looked yet went right to her. I glanced up to the balcony; Drew was waiting there, counting minutes, ready to bolt down the stairs. If we'd been late, he would have yelled for Aubrey to go comfort Aisha, and he would have darted through the portal to find us in 1906 because staying home and grieving was not an option.

When he saw me looking, he waved and then went inside.

"I left him there." Will's voice wavered and came out in a near whisper. "He was wet and tiny and hungry, and I left him there to survive the worst earthquake—"

Aisha pulled him into a tight hug, but she didn't try to tell him it was all right. She held him while he sobbed because his guilt and grief were real, and he needed somewhere to put it all. She waited while he let it leak from his soul so that he would be done before going home, where everyone else would want to help.

I slid off his shoulder and jumped to the ground to wait.

He'd given me this; I gave him time to catch his breath.

"I left a baby to survive on his own, Enzo," he said when they finally pulled apart.

Will.

Will.

Will.

His breath hitched.

He's right here. That baby is right here. He ate rats, and he fought off birds and stupid, mean people, but he survived. And he's right here.

"Wick, I know that, but it still felt wrong."

You have to let things go sometimes, you know that.

He shoved his hands in his pockets and stared at me. He knew the rules, he knew the order of things, but he still wanted to turn around and go back to save the kitten I'd once been.

Why did you save Jax when he rode down California Street on the bike?

"You know why, Wick. His death would have been an anomaly. Time intended for him to live."

Why didn't you save Queen Donna? You could have gone back and told her she was sick before it was too late, but you didn't.

"Because the timeline was clear. She was always supposed..." He took a deep breath. "Wick, I know the timeline, and I know you survived exactly how you were meant to. I can't help how I feel."

Oh, I don't think I was supposed to be there at all. I think someone put me there, and I still want to know why. But I don't want my past changed, not in any loop, not when it leads me to now. Just like you don't want to risk changing anything that gives you Aisha and Jay.

"Even knowing how hard just living day to day was?"

Even. Call it Wick's Grand Adventure. I don't remember most of it, but it's my life, and I'm entitled to it.

Aisha scooped me up and held me tight. "Of course, you are, sweetie. Will is entitled to be sad about it, though."

He reached into the outside pocket on his coat, fishing for the few pieces of metal he'd brought back. I pressed against Aisha, hard. I suddenly had no wish to be anywhere near those things and wanted him to put the pieces back where I couldn't see.

"We found these near him," Will said to Aisha. "They're part of a ship—"

Put them back.

I wiggled in her grasp until she set me down.

Put them back. I don't want to see them.

"They're just puzzle pieces, Wick. A puzzle we need to assemble."

I scooted back until there was enough distance that I didn't feel the terror that had started to bubble in the pit of my stomach.

I know. But put them back. Please. I don't want to see them.

"All right." He slipped them back into his pocket. "Are you okay?"

There was a memory tickling the very center of my brain, and unlike the others, I didn't want this one working its way out. All I wanted was to go home and have a snack and then curl up in front of a fire. It wasn't cold out, but I started to shiver and climbed Aisha's leg until she picked me off it and cuddled me close.

"You can have a fire, sweetie, it's all right," she cooed as we headed for the front door. "You've had a hard day, haven't you? I'll turn the fire on while Will gets some food for you."

"Hell, I'm hungry, too," he grumbled.

I'll share with you. You like tuna, right? We'll have tuna and then sit by the fire, and maybe tomorrow I'll be okay with looking at those things.

*

She made me sleep in bed with them. Without Will saying so, she knew he wanted me close, and sleeping on the window seat was too far away. I curled up at the foot of the bed and slowed my breathing so that he would think I was asleep and not lying awake and afraid, hoping he would be able to sleep, too.

"He's so old," Will whispered into the dark. He was on his back, arms folded behind his head, and Aisha was sitting beside him, resting against the headboard. "In the last year I've gone from thinking he was my age, to realizing he was at least sixty, and now? At the very least, he was a kitten in nineteen-hundred-six. Finn found him sixty years later. At a minimum, Wick is a hundred years old. Probably closer to one-twenty."

"He said he was new. How new?"

"He was small, no doubt, but he wasn't a newborn. His command of language was rudimentary, but that he understood and could speak at all tells me he'd been alive for more than a few weeks. Someone put him there, someone from my birth When."

"You're sure of that."

"The pieces of the ship could have only come from one place. Dad had dozens in different sizes. And his fuel source was unique—the battery we found was one of his."

He found it hard to believe that Finn would have sent me off in one of those ships. When he was testing the smaller machines, the one he used to create the portal in the back of Oz's closet, he'd refused to let me near it. It wasn't worth the risk to me, and he'd devised a hook to reach through and retrieve it. He limited his use of live test subjects, and when he needed one, it was always a person who knew the dangers.

"Someone in his lab, then," she decided. "How many people had access to his inventions?"

Will wasn't sure. There was the actual lab under Union Square, but he'd never counted more than a dozen people at any given time. There was an entire research campus off-site, and it employed thousands.

"I have no idea how many people he gave access to his work with time travel. I'd always assumed it was the select few chosen to work with him and my mother in the lab, but it was all a massive undertaking, and I'm sure I was shielded from most of it."

There was somewhat of a revolving door in the lab; Finn and Jo employed students from several fields, teaching as they created the framework of the portal tunnel. As students graduated and moved on, new people were hired. Some, like Brian Massimo—who had been in this When as long as Will had and was now the royal physician—had shown promise in fields unrelated to physics and had been strongly encouraged to follow their dreams. Most, like Mass, balked; the world was ending, and they wanted—needed—to help save it. But Jo, especially, wanted someone to be there when the world didn't end, and she knew that pursuing studies in engineering and medicine would be vital.

"I was eight, I think, when Mass left to finish his residency. My parents were still in their thirties. Yet in my head, they were all so old." He laughed at himself. "My memories of the techs who made time for me, and who kept me amused, are of solid adults when truthfully, they were in their early twenties. Drew's age."

"He's an adult."

"Well." He sighed then, and his weight on the bed shifted as he sat up. "Wick was already in his seventies then. At least. I still can't shake the notion that I should have scooped Seven up and whisked him through a portal just long enough to avoid the earthquake. His existence would have continued. What if I was meant to?"

"Sweetie." There was some fumbling as she turned to reach something on her nightstand. "Look. This is data from the quake, and the damages incurred. The Ghirardelli factory was left pretty much unscathed and even opened for business again a few days later."

He took the tablet from her and read.

"Wick told Seven to stay there for a reason. He was safe where he was. And even if he doesn't fully remember those days, he may have grasped that Seven needed to stay for the experience. What he learned might have been a valuable survival tool."

"Then leaving him was the right thing."

"Robbing him of that might have meant

condemning him, Will. As hard as it was, he needed to stay put."

I rolled over onto my back, tilting my head back so that I could see him.

Told you.

"You're a nosy little shit."

Yeah, but you love me, and you promised to stuff me with cheese for the rest of my life.

"Do you still want to pursue this, Wick? We can take the ship fragments to my father tomorrow and see what he says."

I still need to know. I'll try to contain myself.

"I'll go with you," Aisha said. "If Wick gets uncomfortable, he and I can raid Finn's fridge or take a walk."

You have to teach tomorrow.

"My students will be fine if I cancel a class."

No. I'll be all right. I can close my eyes if the ship pieces bother me.

"Maybe she wants a day off," Will said.

Life is hard. She'll survive.

*

She went to work. We went to Finn's lab.

Will kept the ship fragments hidden in his backpack until Finn needed to see them, and then he only pulled out one at a time, glancing at me with each one to make sure I was all right. He started with the biggest piece, the one with the attached battery, setting it on the table in the tiny lab kitchen. I waited on the counter while Finn turned it over in his hand, squinting as he tried to examine everything about it. It was one of his designs, he was sure of that, but it wasn't identical to anything he'd built.

"The metals are quite a bit thinner than anything I ever used and the way it seems to have cracked, I'm assuming it was molded and cooled incorrectly. There aren't enough carbon fibers woven into the shell. The battery resembles the solar collection plasma packs I used in my first ship." He held it by the tiny battery, and the four-inch jagged fragment spun on the end of the cable. "It's considerably smaller than the batteries I used."

"Even in the micro-vessels you were playing with?"

The packs he used in the smallest of his ships were still fist-sized. "I didn't need to make them smaller because I didn't leave pilot space inside. I made three of them, but only one was ever used to punch a new portal hole."

"In my boyhood closet."

Finn nodded. "I didn't need anyone in it. It was filled with the computer, engine and fuel packs. Once the portal was opened, I just reached through and grabbed it with a hook."

Will remembered that. He sat outside the closet while Finn built and calibrated the track and then tested it and howled when Finn's arm disappeared up to his shoulder as he reached for the ship. An hour later he sat at the open door to watch as the ship popped through, followed by his father's disembodied arm.

"How old was I?"

"Fifteen," Finn said. "Old enough that it shouldn't have been that funny, young enough that of course, it was."

You didn't laugh about much then. We were all happy you found something funny.

"None of us laughed much then, Wick," Finn said. "I was about to take you to live with baby Jax, and we'd accepted who Will would become. I think I would have walked across Union Square naked if it would have made him smile."

"Mom might have laughed. I would have been horrified."

Finn pushed away from the table and got up. "Yes, says the man who was the boy who had so little modesty that he routinely walked naked from the lab shower into my office and didn't care who saw."

"Blame Mom. I'm still not modest."

You've learned to cover up. You don't walk up and down the stairs at home without pants on.

"Because the Queen would be offended, Wick. We don't offend the Queen, lest the King has us beheaded."

He wouldn't behead you. He'd just have Oz neuter you with a wicked snap front kick.

"Ow."

Finn didn't ask for a translation. "I need to take this downstairs and get a better look. And I can't blame your mother for your lack of modesty, Will. Or did you never notice that she never left the bedroom unless she was dressed?"

"I never thought about it." Will scooped me up and followed Finn into the stairwell. "Then it's your fault. Perverted old man, wandering the house in his underwear."

"Yes, I was ancient," Finn snorted. "You know, when you plucked Jax off the bridge, I was only two years older than you are now. Four older than when you left home. If I was old, guess what. So are you."

"I'm not even middle-aged, Dad. You were ancient, regardless."

"Yeah, love you, too."

He led us to the fourth level of the lab. Tucked into a corner was an enclosure that looked a lot like the fish tank the vet Will took me to every year had on display, but this one was long, narrow, and empty, with a top and a little door in the front. Finn took the fragments from Will and set them inside, and then made sure the door was locked and sealed tight before flipping a switch that set its computer programming in motion.

"I should be able to determine how old these pieces are and what the battery is comprised of," he said absently, poking at the computer keyboard.

"What did you do with discarded materials?" Will asked. "If you set aside a failed design, could someone else have used it?"

"Discarded ships were melted down and retooled for other equipment, and I can account for each one we retained. One is here—" he gestured to the ceiling, meaning it was on another level "—and the rest are stored here in the future. I would have noticed if one were missing."

"Could one of your techs have built one without your input?"

"Possibly," Finn allowed. "But building it and having the means to launch are different things. It requires a considerable amount of power, and the track it runs on requires precision."

"Yet you operated one in the closet."

"To open a portal. I can open one that size with minimal space. This was clearly used for direct time transport, and to launch a ship so small into null space? That requires a meticulously laid out track. It's honestly easier to send off a bigger one. The difference between hitting a target with a bomb over a jellybean."

Any number of Finn's employees had the knowledge to build and launch a ship, but none had access to the track without his permission. Manufacturing a track of their own was virtually impossible, simply because the amount of power needed to operate the track couldn't be easily obtained. It wasn't a simple matter of plugging something in; the mechanical structures and electrical requirements made the gate Will built on the Bay Bridge look like a toy. Finn hadn't needed one when he'd opened the tiny closet portal for me; construction of the portal tunnel had been completed and thoroughly tested, and he wasn't bouncing the ship off null space. He only needed to punch a hole in time, big enough to allow me easy passage. After that, the ships went into storage.

"The only time I've taken one out was to open the portal in the hospital," Finn said. "The ship went back into storage as soon as we knew that it was functional on both sides."

"And it was far too large to be this one," Will mused.

"That was a fun one to ride in. I stopped half an inch from the end of the corridor. Rod swears your mother shrieked."

"She was probably concerned with damage to the hospital and the resulting liability."

"Really, Dash, I'm going to start taking the insults personally."

Will leaned over and kissed Finn's temple. "I love you, you know that."

Finn didn't have time to come up with an insult of his own. The computer beeped, and data began scrolling on the monitor. They stood shoulder to shoulder as they read it together, and I tried to follow it from my perch on Will's shoulder, but it scrolled past too quickly for me to read.

"That's not a battery pack," Finn said. "It's a data drive. The black box, so to speak."

"Then we might be able to access the files on it."

"I hope so." Finn leaned in closer to the monitor. "Hell, Will, the dating on the metal puts it a hundred fifty years or so before I built my first ship."

Will opened the little door and fished out the piece with the cable attached. "That might explain how thin the metal is. Whoever built it didn't have the specs that would allow it to hold together through null space."

"You're presuming it went through null space. People have been trying to solve time from the moment they grasped that we all seemingly flow in one direction. Someone may have found a way, but never knew it. If they launched something and it never came back?"

"They didn't launch something. They launched Wick."

"No point in getting your shorts in a knot right now," Finn said as he took the fragment from Will. "Let's crack this puppy open and see what's inside."

8

Finn needed time to open the casing on the tiny data drive—he didn't want to risk damaging anything inside—and it was time to meet Aisha at the little corner bakery on Union Square, so we left everything with him and left to meet her. Every day that he could, when she was done teaching her last class at the university, Will took a break from work, or he ended his day, and they met for coffee. It was a slice of quiet when they talked about their day and made plans for the next, though sometimes Aubrey joined them, and they sat outside until dinner time, planning out their kids' lives and laughing at the notion that they had any real say about it.

The one thing Aubrey wanted most was for them to all choose to stay close. Oz and Drew were living in the combined space of her and Zed's bedrooms, with the idea that once they were finished with school and contemplating a family, they would move upstairs to the remodeled guest suite across the hall from Will and Aisha. Eli had already taken Will's old apartment downstairs, and Drew's had been remodeled for either Zed or Jay to move into, and she was determined to create more space for at least one more.

She might not be able to plan out their relationships and careers, but she was certain she could keep her family in one spot. Will thought it was possible, even though he brushed off my warning that everyone living in the building together made them one giant tasty target for political dinosaurs to hunt. Aisha just wanted Jay to be happy, no matter where he was.

Aisha was already at the bakery, sitting at a table outside with a cup of coffee for him, tea for her, and bacon for me.

The people that worked at the bakery liked me and always saved me a slice of bacon from the meat made for their breakfast sandwiches. Will never had to pay for it, they just gave it to him, and in turn, he made sure he tipped well.

"I wasn't sure you'd make it today," she said, sliding the coffee cup across the table to him. "I hoped, but I wasn't counting on it."

You should have waited to buy his coffee then. But I'm not complaining about the bacon. Bacon keeps.

Will explained what they'd done so far. "It's twenty-seventh-century technology, built in the twenty-fifth century. Dad's poking through the ship's computer, and I hope to hell he doesn't discover that someone he trusted brought his data back and tried to beat him to the punch with it."

You mean like you're doing by helping Drew build a holographic simulator? And all the nanobot thingies?

"Hush. And I didn't bring tech from the future. Drew's building everything himself. I'm simply nudging him in the right direction."

Still. It's okay for you to push the timeline in another direction but not someone else.

"Exactly."

"Sweetie, Will just doesn't want someone stealing his dad's hard work. He's allowed to be biased."

"It's more than that. Anyone trying to change what my father did would also be changing the efforts he made to save the world. Anyone with access to his data knew what he was doing. That's what I have issue with. First and foremost, he was trying to save this planet, and if he couldn't do that, then he wanted to save as many people as possible. Interfering with that could mean the end of everything."

I'm still going to yank on your shorts. You were doing it to Finn, you know.

Will's phone pinged and he picked it up. "Yank away, Wick." He read his text and then said to Aisha, "The Queen has requested our company for dinner."

"Requested or ordered?"

"She said, and I quote, 'You're all coming to dinner tonight. I'm in the mood for burgers and beer. Bring beer.'" He set the phone down. "You know what she really wants."

"Beer, apparently."

"You're about to get grilled regarding your birthday, and what kind of cake you want at the party you have not asked for but are clearly getting."

She brightened. "Oh, fun. I haven't had a party in years."

"Then you should have a party. Let Aubrey run with it. She delights in arranging these things, and you'll have a much nicer time than you would were I left to the planning."

There's gonna be a lot of balloons.

"Or," Aisha said, "she'll suggest we all head back for twenty-six-seventeen for fajitas and head-sized margaritas."

"I'll drink yours."

"How sweet of you." She leaned toward him for a kiss. "Maybe my birthday is a good time to tell everyone. I'll be three months along by then."

"Are we ready to share this?"

"It still gives us a couple of weeks to savor the secret. Besides, my students are getting suspicious. I hurled my poor toenails into a trash can today. Drew quietly got up and set a handful of mints on my desk and offered to go get me some tea and crackers."

"He knows, then. He came prepared with mints."

"He's at least assuming."

The corners of Will's mouth tugged up. "He's good at keeping secrets, but perhaps this one isn't fair. He wants us to have a baby almost as much as we want to have a baby. I think he intends to practice on ours before he and Oz have one." His phone pinged again. "Dad."

She wanted to get Finn a cup of coffee before we headed back to the lab, so Will got it while she waited. When he came back, as she got up, she asked, "Tell everyone tonight, then? Rescue poor Drew from biting his tongue too hard?"

"If my parents are going to be there, why not?"

"If they're not?"

He jabbed the elevator button. "Then it needs to wait. We can't tell everyone else and not them."

She dug into her pocket for her phone. "Then we're telling them now. I'm calling Jo to meet us here. They should be the first to know."

*

Their excitement waned halfway across the lab floor, when they spotted Finn in his office. He was at his desk, eyebrows furrowed, fist held to his mouth the way people do when they're sullen and contemplating things they don't want to think about. He heard us but didn't turn, and when Will was at the doorway, he lowered his hand and sighed, "This isn't good."

"What did you find?" He set me on the desk and then dragged chairs away from the wall for Aisha and himself. "Did someone appropriate your work?"

"Probably not." He pointed to the monitor. He had two sets of data running side by side. "The column on the left is data from the ship fragments you found. The one on the right is from my ship. The ship I was stranded in."

"Intermittent blips," Will said. "Power interruptions or static interference?"

Finn dug a laser pointer out of a drawer and pointed it at the data on the right. "This is from the moment I landed in twenty-fifteen. And this—" he scrolled down a dozen lines "—is the moment I hit my transponder and sent myself into null space. Every dotted line after that corresponds to twenty years. It picks back up when the ship unstuck itself and landed in twenty-four-fifteen."

He pointed to the other side of the screen. "Other than the sequencing—I shot myself into the ship with the transponder and the other was launched—the timing nearly lines us up. The smaller ship was stuck in null space, as well." He scrolled both columns, looking for the thing he wanted Will to see. "The sensors from my ship picked up an anomaly, something I saw but discarded as being static. It was too small to be anything, and I couldn't contact it regardless."

"Wick's ship had to bounce off null space," Will mused.

"No, look at the lines, Will. He entered null space at roughly the same time, give or take a dozen years, and he left it soon after I did."

"Dad, you were stuck there for four hundred years."

His head moved, just a bit, a tight nod that I felt like a punch to my stomach. "I felt every moment of it, Dash. It was almost kinder when I had no memory."

In the seconds it took that to sink in for Will,

Aisha was out of her chair, snatching me off the desk for an ill-timed hug.

"Wick was stuck there with you," Will breathed.

"Nearly every goddamned, horrible minute of it."

I wiggled out of Aisha's grasp. My skin was twitching, tiny bugs that I couldn't see biting my haunches, and I needed to get away from it. I scrambled over her shoulder and leaped to the floor, and I ran.

There was nowhere to go. I bolted for the tiny kitchen and jumped onto the table, then to the counter and ran the length of it. When there was no more counter, I jumped down and circled the room, and no matter how many times Will told me it was all right, I couldn't shake the tiny things snapping at me.

If I stopped, they would win. With every electric snap to my skin, I was sure of it. Tiny things banding together were like the pigeons on Union Square. If I gave them a chance, even a small one, they would eat me. Everything I had ever been afraid of was nipping at me, and if I stopped running the nips would turn into bites, and the bites would turn me into a meal.

On my third run of the room, he snatched me up.

No, no, no, no, no, no no.

"Wick."

No. Let me go. It's not fair.

"You don't remember it—"

No, no, no. It's not fair. Let me go.

He didn't let me go. He tried to pull me closer, and the moisture of his breath on my head felt like tiny wet knives on my ears. I wanted down, I didn't want to be held. I wanted to run until my life stopped hurting.

Let me go. Everything is biting me.

"It's all right, Wick. You're all—"

Nothing is all right. Let me go.

I didn't think about it. All I wanted was down so that I could run away.

I bit him.

Without thinking about it, I sunk my teeth into his arm. I was trapped and had no way out, so I bit down as hard as I could.

He didn't flinch.

Aisha's hand shot forward, and she gasped, but Will stood still and didn't even twitch, and he didn't yell at me. When my mouth filled with the taste of his blood, I let go and then buried my face against his chest.

I didn't mean to.

"I know. It's all right."

It's not fair. I don't want to live forever. It's not fair. It's not fair, it's not fair.

"We don't know that you will, Wick. I know a hundred seems like forever—"

Five hundred.

Finn was in null space for four hundred years, and we know he lives until he's at least three hundred. That means the extra old Finn we met in the other When was seven hundred years old. Those years count.

"Dad," Will said helplessly.

"Liam Finnegan is healthy and sharp. He shows no real signs of slowing down. I already knew that's what I was headed for."

It's not fair. I shouldn't have to live forever.

"I'll be here with you," Finn said.

But you remember. Your brain remembers. Mine forgets. I'm tired of forgetting.

"I don't want you to remember null space, Wick," Finn said. "Not a tiny bit of it."

It was one blink, one breath, one heartbeat, and it took four hundred years.

Aisha pulled me away from Will so that she could clean his wound, and I got the first look at what I'd done to him. Blood ran down his arm and splattered on the floor, leaving spots on his shoes and pants. His shirt was stained in red where I'd rubbed my face. She set me on the center island, and no one said anything about the streaks of Will's blood I wiped across the metal countertop with my tail.

I didn't mean to hurt you. I'm sorry.

"It doesn't hurt, Wick," Will lied. "I know you didn't mean to do this."

Finn crouched low so that his face was near mine. "Listen to me. We know I'm still going to be here in two hundred years. Will might live just as long. We will *always* make sure you have someone."

"I had this talk with him already, Dad," Will said. Aisha was wiping his arm with a wet cloth, and I know it hurt, but he didn't show it. "We have an agreement. I don't like it, but I promised him that when we're old, old men, if he's ready to move on, I'll help him."

"And that's your right," Finn said to me. "If Will dies before you're ready, I'll honor his promise, okay? I swear that to you."

The lab door clicked as Jo came in. "What the hell are you agreeing to, Finn?"

He straightened. "When we are both impossibly old, if Wick is ready to rest, I'll help him."

She saw the blood on the floor. "What happened? Will?"

I bit him. I'm sorry.

"Wick got a bit excited, that's all. It was just a tiny nip."

You just lied to your mom, dude. She knows it. I bit you hard. Tell her I said I'm sorry because I really am.

She brushed past Aisha and grabbed a first aid kit from the cupboard, fishing a roll of gauze and some tape out of it. After Aisha had washed and covered the bite in antiseptic, she let Jo roll the gauze on while she cleaned up the mess I'd made on the island and the floor.

"Why," Jo wanted to know, "would Wick think there will come a time when he's ready to let go? Think of everything to come. All the generations of Blackshear babies that will love him as much as we do."

Tell them. Please. Make this all better and tell them.

"Right now, Wick?" Will asked, reaching out to rub the top of my head.

Please. They're looking at me and I'm sorry and I want everyone to be happy.

"No one is upset with you, Wick. You were frightened. I understand why it happened."

But they're looking at me and I can't tell them I'm sorry, and they'll be happy if you tell them now. Please.

"You think Wick will do well with infants?" Will asked. "Tiny people chasing him around, squealing and screaming, and all the crying?"

"He has you to run to," Finn snorted. "Once Oz and Drew have kids, Wick might move in with you full time."

"Or," Aisha said carefully, "he'll want to move in with Oz and Drew instead. Soon. Before the end of fall."

It took a few heartbeats for that to sink in.

"No," Jo breathed. "Don't tease me. Don't joke about that. Please be serious."

"We would no' tease you about that," Will said, his voice a soft Scottish whisper.

It was Aisha Jo reached for. She squealed and hugged her daughter-in-law, and it was everything she could do to keep from jumping up and down.

Finn rooted in place, and his breath came in several huge gulps as he failed to hold back the tears. He croaked, "Dash," and then buried his face against Will's shoulder, grabbing Will's bloody shirt with both hands.

"He's happy," Will assured Aisha.

"Happy as hell," Jo said. "He's always wanted this for you, Will. Even when it seemed impossible."

"You're the first to know," Will said as he planted a kiss on Finn's head. "Well, other than Jay. He's known for a while."

"How far along?" Jo asked. "When are you due?"

Thank you for telling them. It's a shame they're not excited about this.

"Late September or early October," Aisha answered.

That spurred Finn into letting go of Will so that he could count on his fingers. "Ah, nice. Oz and Drew have a honeymoon, and you have the honeymoon baby."

They had fun in the park with the Tree of Life and stars and frogs that I chased. And the bunny I made friends with.

Wait. That's not the rabbit that died, right?

"That's just an old expression," Will said to me. "No rabbits were harmed in the conception of this child."

Finn crinkled his nose. "They used to actually kill rabbits in pregnancy tests."

That made both Jo and Aisha cringe.

Will skipped right over the gruesome idea. "We're telling everyone else at dinner tonight. So no slip of the tongue, all right?"

They had been invited but had already made plans with Eli. Finn told Will to take a case of his beer from the lab fridge and celebrate hard. "But not you," he said to Aisha. "Tell them early, before they start pushing the booze on you."

"Tell Mom about the ship," Will said as we headed for the door. "Show her the data."

"I'll look at it some more," he said, "but the big question won't be in those files. We still don't know who put Wick in the ship in the first place."

Will had an idea, but it would have to wait.

He had people to thrill first.

9

"Greetings from my father, with apologies that he and my mother could not be here," Will said as he carried the case of Finn's personal brew into the kitchen. "This is horrible beer, truly, no one should have to suffer for it. I'll drink it and spare you all."

"Yeah, no." Jax grabbed a bottle out of the case. "Finn needs to retire from tinkering with universal Armageddon type things and open his own brewery. I swear, if he does, I'll name him as the official royal brewmaster."

Aubrey made him put the beer back because he had to help carry food to the roof. The kids were already there; they'd set up the firepit, and Jax had trusted Drew with his grill. It hurt, but he'd allowed Drew to fire it up. "He's not grilling the burgers, but I let him touch my precious," Jax snorted.

"Ew."

"What's that from, anyway? It rings a bell."

"Tolkien. The Hobbit. Lord of the Rings. And you sound far creepier than Gollum ever did."

Aubrey assured them that they were both creepy, and poked Jax to head for the elevator.

The summer before, for Oz's birthday, Will and Drew built the framework for a tent of lights and no one wanted to take it down when the party was over. It was used often. Zed took Sophia to the roof a few times to dance under the lights. Jax and Aubrey sometimes chased the kids away so they could do the same thing, alone, without guards. Aisha had proposed to Will under the lights, on Oz's birthday. Oz and Drew lounged under the lights just to talk. When Drew's parents came for his wedding and their shuttle clipped and broke the frame, he and Will re-built it, because the lights made them happy.

It probably didn't give people who lived in nearby buildings warm, fuzzy feelings, but Aubrey said there had been no complaints, so we were still allowed to use them.

"Who's going to complain that the King and Queen have lights on the roof and turn them on a couple times a week?" Zed pointed out. "It's not like they're going to march up to the front door and tell the twenty-year-old guard on duty that it's royally pissing them off."

"Are you kidding?" Oz countered. "Some of them would open a window and yell at us. Using a megaphone. They don't care who we are."

They probably cared, a little bit.

It wasn't dark out yet, but they'd already turned the lights and the fire pit on. Soft music floated from a speaker set up in the closest corner, and they'd set all the chairs in a circle around the fire pit because that's how Jax and Aubrey liked it. I liked it, too, because I could walk the rim of the pit—it wasn't real fire, so I wouldn't go up in flames like a furry little torch—and I could see everyone.

That was handy when they were eating. I could run the rim and get bites of burger and cheese and was only told no when I'd eaten enough to make someone worry that I would either vomit or pop.

When Jax went to throw the burgers on the grill, Will asked him to throw on an extra. "Wick's had a hard day. He deserves his own."

Jax gestured to the bandage around Will's forearm. "Anything to do with that?"

"Somewhat. He was upset and frightened. He bit me. He's apologized."

"What the hell? Wick's never been a biter."

"Like I said, he's had a hard day. He was upset, and we're not angry with him, all right?"

Jax looked down at me. "Bite me, and I turn you inside out, got it?"

Liar.

You love me.

"He had a good reason for biting you?" Jax asked Will.

"He did, and I'll explain later. Suffice to say, he had every right to be out of sorts."

"But you're all right now?" he asked me. "That's all that matters. Will can suffer."

I'll be better when I can have my burger.

"Try to not think about it," Will whispered as he picked me up. "Tonight, we need to relax."

When are you telling them?

"Soon. I need to talk to Aisha first."

When he sat in the chair next to her, he slid his hand down her arm, tapping his middle finger against her palm just before their fingers intertwined. Their conversation took place silently, and several times faster than if they'd spoken out loud to each other.

Kiss her.

"Why, Wick?"

Because I like it when you kiss her. And if you kiss her, it'll distract Jax from the beer bottle he's about to hand her.

Jax was fishing around in the cooler, and a second later he leaned over the fire pit with two beers in hand. "It's a shame Finn isn't here to hear how awful you think his beer is."

Will took them both, then offered one to Oz.

"Hey!" Jax tried to grab the bottle from her, but she held it out of his reach, wiggling it to taunt him. "Fine. If you're old enough to be married, you're old enough for a beer, but don't get drunk. I'm not ready to see that. One, that's it. Finn brews strong."

"Note, he didn't offer me one," Drew said, pretending offense.

Jax snorted. "You're a big boy. The cooler's right there. If you want one, get one. Aubrey?"

She sat back in her chair, arms folded. "No, I think I'm going to abstain with Aisha. It's such a rarity."

"Is not," Aisha snickered.

"Sweetie, I've never seen you turn down a good drink when the boys are hammering them back."

"Sure, make me sound like I have a problem. They love Finn's beer. I'm just being nice and letting them have it all."

Drew laughed and coughed out a word on Aubrey's list under his breath.

"She hasn't been drinking lately, has she?" Jax asked of no one in particular. "I offered my best scotch the other night, and she turned her nose up at it. I think we should be offended. We're clearly not her drinking buddies anymore."

"Maybe you just drink too much," Jay offered.

"Hey. Shut up." Jax pointed his bottle at Jay. "On the other hand, Will's gotten Oz drunk before. Want a beer?"

When Aisha didn't immediately say no, Jay's mouth opened, then closed, then he said, "Um, I don't even know if I like beer."

"Son, if your mother's eyes could roll any harder, they'd sound like marbles on tile."

"When would I have had beer?"

"When did your dad install a lock on his fridge?" Aisha asked. "Or his liquor cabinet? Don't try to b.s. me, Jay. I know he lets you have one every now and then."

"Only, like, half a glass. I swear. He said not to tell you, just in case it ticked you off. And it wasn't until, ah, puberty hit, so it's not like—"

"I don't mind, Jay. Just use some common sense, all right?"

He took the bottle from Jax. "I won't finish it. I don't want to waste it."

"Share, then. Zed? Half a beer, no more."

I don't think Zed wanted it because his lip curled the way people do when something stinks. "Ugh. I'm with Drew. Most alcohol tastes horrible."

"You've had beer before," Jax said.

"I know. I've had just enough to know that I tried it because I wasn't old enough and drinking it made me feel like I was badass. I'm old enough now to admit that I don't like it."

"Fair enough. Jay, just give the second half to Will or me."

"We still haven't addressed Aisha's new aversion to alcohol," Aubrey said.

"Give her a break," Drew said. "I know she was feeling like crap earlier. She barfed in front of the entire class this morning. Yesterday, too. And the day—"

"You're not helping," Will said.

"Am, too." He looked at Aisha. "I'll make sure to have plenty of mints on hand Monday. Should I bring crackers, too? I can stop before class and get you some hot tea."

Jax pointed at Drew. "You, be quiet." Then at Will. "You, start talking. Are we?"

He tried to not smile. I could see it tugging at the corners of his mouth, that *oh-yeah-I-did* grin that he wanted to hold onto for just a few seconds more, but he lost the battle in under three seconds. "Indeed," Will answered. "We are."

"Get up, loser," Jax ordered. He sprang out of his chair to hug Will, and the next thing I knew my field of vision was nothing but people's legs and one unfortunate moment when all I had in my field of vision was Drew's butt.

It took Aubrey a long time to let go of Aisha. "I knew it, I knew it," she squealed. "Not because you weren't drinking, but you've been damn near glowing, and Will is so...settled."

"Content," Will said.

"Oh, hon, you were content when she married you. It was something else." She turned her hugs on him and gave him a kiss. "It's like the air around you sighed happily."

Told you.

"Wick felt that, too. He said he heard my soul sigh when Aisha became an anchor."

"Wait." They all sat back down, but Jax perched on the edge of his seat. "Seriously. That can happen? You can basically flip anchors?"

"Some people have successfully changed anchors. I'm now fortunate enough to have two. My link to Wick did not sever."

"Three, I think," Aubrey said. "You're a lucky man, Will."

"Indeed."

"And I finally get to be a big brother," Jay said. "You people are never getting me to move out now."

Jax pointed his bottle again. "You move out, and you upset the Queen. There are laws about that. I banish or behead anyone who upsets the Queen. The best you can hope for is to share the apartment downstairs with Zed."

"It's ready now," Zed said. "When do we get to move in?"

"When you're twenty-one. Unless you're grounded, then when you're thirty."

While Zed and Jay pretended to argue with Jax about that, Will took the chance to steal a long, quiet kiss. I jumped onto his lap and head-butted them both in the chin and then curled up. At least for the rest of the night, I wasn't going to think about how old I really was, where I'd come from, or who put me there. Everyone was five kinds of happy—Jay might have been six because that beer was getting to him—and it was hard to be upset when everyone important to me was celebrating.

Even Drew wanted to celebrate. There was a small bottle of cinnamon whiskey in the cooler, the one boozy drink he really liked, and he wanted it.

"Mr. B," he said, stretching to see past Oz, "hand me the bottle?"

"No."

"No? All right, fine, I'll get it myself."

"No." Jax sat back and folded his arms. "I've told you half a dozen times to call me by name. Do it." He pointed at Jay. "You, too."

Jay's mouth hung open but Drew just sighed. "Come on. Years of habit."

"Do it."

"Fine. Jax, would you please hand me the whiskey bottle?"

He fished it from the bottom of the cooler and tossed it to Drew, then turned to Jay. "And you. Do it."

"But I already have a drink. And it's weird."

"Don't bully him," Will said. "Jay, is it the familiarity that bothers you, or simply propriety?"

"I don't know. I can get used to a new name. I got used to mine. I'm getting used to yours."

"Eh? What are you calling him?" Jax asked.

"Dad. But most of the time it comes out Willlllldad."

"Fine. I laid claim to him as a brother, and my father adopted him. That makes you my nephew. Uncle Jax, then. By order of the King."

"He's not wearing the crown, sweetie," Aubrey said to Jay. "It's a request, not an order. But we would be so honored if you would."

"Yeah, yeah, all right. I'd like that, I really would. But I'll trip up a lot." He snorted, hard, and said, "You're gonna be Mr. Beeeeeuncle Jax for a while."

"Oh, this is awesome," Oz blurted. "This means I get to call Will Uncle Willie now!"

"You will not."

"Unca Willie." She jabbed Drew with her elbow. "Hey, we're going to be great, great grandparents before we even become parents. How cool is that?"

"Your family tree must look like a knotted vine," Jay mused.

Will chuckled. "Just some drooping branches."

Jay thought about it, and then said to Oz, "You all realize that one day this kid will grow up and wind up marrying one of your kids, and Will's gonna be, like, his own uncle or something."

"We'll burn that bridge when we get to it," Will said.

Aubrey raised an eyebrow and asked Oz, "So, when are we becoming grandparents?"

"Oh, god." Oz sighed and looked at Will. "This is your fault. She's going to be nothing but *babies* for the next year. By the time my birthday rolls around, she'll be banging on our door yelling, 'Give me grandchildren! Get to it!'"

"Good thing she doesn't have the throne," Zed said. "She'd issue a royal proclamation, and then you'd have to."

"Maybe after I finish school," Drew told Aubrey. "If we have one before then, the King will string me up by things I don't want a string wrapped around."

"Eh," Jax grunted. "You're married now. I don't care. Have a kid if you want. Will's going to be backing off work for a while anyway. He can babysit while you get the degree you promised me."

"Not a discussion I was expecting to have yet," Will said.

Jax had expected that when Oz and Drew decided to start a family, Will would ask to curtail his schedule somewhat. He'd done it when Oz was born, and it was no secret that he'd made the offer to Drew more than once. "You're going part-time with a baby of your own, I get that. I expect that." He turned to Oz. "Learn a little more of what Will does, sweetheart. If you take up even a fraction of his duties, just some of the meetings he engages in on my behalf, we'll make the rest work."

"Will actually works?" Drew snorted.

It took almost an hour before they stopped picking on Will. After a while, I realized Will kept looking at Zed because he was the only one not finding things to mock. He was quiet; he ate his burger, and he laughed a lot, but he didn't find anything to make fun of Will about.

While Jax scraped the grill clean and Drew was stacking everyone's dirty plates, Will switched chairs to sit near him, and asked if he was all right.

"Tired, that's all."

"You look more concerned than tired."

"I worked until three this morning, got to bed at four, and then had to be up at eight for my first class. My eyeballs are burning like crazy. Right now, all I want is to go to bed."

"Then go."

"Once I'm sure Mom has had the dinner she wanted. She seemed like she really wanted everyone here."

"She's had what she wanted. Are you sure it's just fatigue?"

"What else would it be?"

"How's Sophia?" Will asked.

Zed's eyes narrowed with suspicion. "All right, what are you getting at, Will? She's fine. I'm fine. We're fine. She's not here tonight because she and Zara had plans."

"Did you ever make an appointment with Mass?"

"Holy hell. No, I didn't. She took care of it, so stop worrying."

Will glanced behind him to make sure Jax was still at the grill, and that Aubrey was out of earshot. Then, very quietly, he said, "I have wrestled with this for a long time. I'm not suggesting it to be pushy. I'm suggesting it because I need to. And you need to listen."

"I've listened to you for years— Wait. What?"

"See Mass soon, Zed."

Zed considered it, then sat up straighter and leaned a little closer to Will. "You're saying the Zed in your history knocked Sophia up? Like, *now?*"

"Not quite yet. And I considered never mentioning it. That—"

"Why the hell wouldn't you? That could screw me up in a major way."

"That child was also very loved, and that Zed handled it well. He excelled at fatherhood, and I suspect you would, as well. But who knows what else he could have become if he'd had the option to wait a few more years?"

"I don't want a kid right now. Please tell me it's not too late."

"A year—"

He wasn't listening. "Jesus. I can't ask her to take a test because another me was too lazy to get a freaking implant. She knows about some of the craziness, Will, but not all of it."

"Just make an appointment with Mass."

That was all Zed needed; he told everyone he was exhausted and needed to call it a night, and then went downstairs to call her. Aisha watched him leave and then settled into his vacated chair and asked what had happened.

"Crisis of conscience," he said. "I told him about my great uncle Zed's first parental surprise, and suggested he do something to prevent that from happening now."

"And now he's panicking, thinking it might be too late."

"Indeed."

"That's a little mean, Will," she said, even though it amused her. "What's he going to say to her? 'I have news from the future, and it needs diapers?'"

"Huh. I should have suggested that."

She reached over the arm of the chair for his hand. "It just got real, Bilbo. They all know now."

"Let the smothering begin."

*

"I really thought that when we told everyone, the secret little bubble we were in would pop." Aisha snuggled against Will, her head on his shoulder. I was on his chest and wiggled until her hand was on my head, scratching absently behind my ears. "It didn't pop. It just got bigger."

"Set boundaries," Will warned. "If you don't, the bubble will smother you with well-intentioned endless dinners and a bottomless cookie jar."

"Jay would certainly like that."

"I'm not remotely kidding, Aisha. Aubrey will go into super-mother mode, and she'll make it her mission in life to make sure you have more food than you'd normally eat in three days in front of you, and she'll follow it up with things you surely must be craving. By royal proclamation, we'll be required to have dinner with them every night, and she'll stuff you with everything she craved when she was pregnant. Mounds of mashed potatoes and fried chicken followed by ice cream with chunks of grapes and crushed breakfast cereal on top. And the volume of tea—"

She sat up sharply. "Oh, god, no more food talk."

I slid off Will's chest because I knew what happened next.

"You don't want to hear about six gallons of tea with three inches of sugar—"

She shot out of bed. Will chuckled under his breath and swung his legs over the side of the mattress and told me to stay put.

I was not staying put. There was a fifty-fifty chance she was going to barf on him, and the odds that she would end up throwing something at him were just as good, and I didn't want to miss that. I followed at his heels and then jumped onto the edge of the tub while she rid herself of dinner and a good part of lunch, too.

While she tried to invert her stomach, Will grabbed two washcloths and soaked them with cold water, then sat on the floor, leaning against the tub, waiting. A minute and a few dry heaves later, she sat next to him, her head resting on the edge of the tub. He laid one washcloth over her forehead, and with the other, he wiped off her chin and lips.

She didn't get it all over, dude. She's clean enough.

Oh. I get it. You're trying to be all gentlemanly. You're not very good at it.

"Can I get you anything?" he asked.

"If you recite a list of food…"

"Something to calm your stomach? A back rub? Run a bath?"

Offer to make oatmeal. That's bland. And it's food. She'll hurl all over again.

"Cool shower," she sighed. "I'm sweating like crazy."

I didn't think women could have hot flashes while they're pregnant.

The sound of Will snorting was almost covered by the movement he made as he got up to turn the shower on. "Sonic or water?"

"Water. And what the hell did Wick say?"

"He thinks you need oatmeal." He helped her up. "I can make that happen. One large, steaming bowl of bland beige paste."

"You're both horrible."

He sat on the edge of the tub with me while she sat on the floor of the shower and let the water pour over her face. She looked miserable, and he looked like he was trying to not smile, which was a little bit mean but I understood why.

"Only a few more weeks of this," he said, sounding hopeful.

Isn't there a drug or something that will make her feel better?

"She's opted not to take anything, Wick. Her choice."

You might want to make better choices, lady.

"Wick, I hear the snark. I swear, I will pull you into the shower with me."

She's kinda mean, too.

How long until she wrinkles? More than usual, I mean.

Aisha stuck her arm out of the shower and flicked water at me. "It's all in the tone, sunshine. I know when you're being a furry little jerk."

Will assured her I was only worried that she would shrivel like a prune if she stayed in the shower too long, and then grabbed a giant, fluffy towel for her. She said she felt better, but was cold, and would appreciate it if he would crawl into bed and warm her up. He pulled all his clothes off and slid between the sheets with her, but there was nothing bouncy about it; all she wanted was to steal his warms, and he was fine with that.

He pulled her close, and only whined a little bit about how cold her skin was now. "Earlier I was going to ask if you felt better and wanted to go with me tomorrow, but I'm guessing the answer is no."

"Depends. Where are you going?"

"Tracking down the person who built the ship that left Wick in nineteen-hundred-six."

She pulled back to look at his face. "How would you even do that?"

"Drew."

"Sweetheart, Drew had nothing to do with that."

"Not our Drew. Older Drew. If anyone could have gotten access to the data necessary to build that ship, it's him."

"He wouldn't."

"Not intentionally," Will said. "But he did work with Jo for a while, and they sent small animals into null space to test her theories about what created my abilities."

Ask older Jo.

"I can't ask her, Wick. She's gone."

Go to when she was alive.

He patted the mattress, inviting me to come closer. "Wick, if I visit her at any point after my death and before hers, it changes her last moments and those were important to both of us."

You change things all the time.

"It would break his heart," Aisha said.

Okay. We'll go see old Drew. But if he did it on purpose, I'm peeing on him.

"Fair enough."

You can pee on him, too.

"You know what, Wick? If it was intentional, I just might."

10

The first place Will headed when we stepped over thirty years into the future was Finn's lab. No one would be surprised to see us there; we visited often, short trips that began a year earlier when Drew asked Will to go forward to tell him— well, everyone—that in the next loop of time, he lived. Drew knew it would matter to them, and the fulfillment of his inebriated request (his first real buzz, thanks to an introduction to cinnamon whiskey by Will and Aisha) confirmed one of Will's theories: changes made in our When didn't change their When. Time erased and overwrote itself as it moved forward in its current loop, but there was no domino effect.

Will had changed major things in his own past; he'd stepped back a few days to save Oz from drowning when she was six, and he'd saved Jax's and Drew's lives. The memories went with him— he clearly remembered the tragedies that spurred him into making those changes, but his life went on as if they'd never happened.

He didn't examine it too closely.

I still wasn't sure he was right.

Finn was where Will expected him to be: hunched over an electronic reading tablet at his office desk, his nose less than a foot from the screen. He was used to people coming and going, so the click of the lab's door didn't stir his interest, and it gave Will a few moments to quietly watch this older version of his father.

"You know, you can get that near-sightedness fixed," he finally said. "It doesn't hurt."

Finn twitched, and when he realized it was Will, his grin snapped fast and he jumped from his seat. "Dash!"

Old Finn had shrunk a bit, enough that when Will hugged him, he could plant a kiss on the top of his head. I stretched forward so that I could headbutt his face, and he rewarded me with a quick tickle of my chin.

"What were you so focused on?" Will asked. "Finally creating the invisible cloak that I wanted when I was five? I still want it, you know."

"Aubrey's chocolate chip banana bread recipe," Finn snorted.

"Ah, you're cooking now."

"Baking. I cooked when you were little. You wouldn't eat it, but I cooked."

I wouldn't eat it, either. He has Aisha's mad cooking skills. He's better than Jo, but still.

How did we survive your childhood?

We followed Finn into the little kitchen, where he proudly showed Will a cake he'd baked. It was lopsided and cracking in the center, and the top layer had slid an inch away from the bottom.

Frosting oozed over the rim of the plate, leaving little dots of sticky chocolate goodness on the counter.

"From scratch!" he boasted.

"I'm impressed." Will wasn't lying. It was cake, and in his universe, there was no such thing as a bad cake. It was one of the few sweet things he liked. Still, he declined when Finn offered him a slice; he'd just had breakfast and was no degree of hungry, but perhaps later.

"I'll hold you to that. Now, are you here to mock my baking abilities or did you need something?"

"Why not both?" Will warned me he was about to pull the ship fragment from his sweatshirt pocket. "This is my current obsession. I'm attempting to track down the person who built it."

Finn took it from him, squinting as he studied it. "Looks like it could be a piece of one of mine."

"It's too thin to be yours." Will touched the edge with his pointy finger. "It shattered, which tells me it was also too brittle to be something you designed."

"Eh." He turned it over. "Did I run tests on this?"

"You did. You determined it was built a good century and a half before you built your first vessel. The small pod—" he touched the dangling tiny egg "—isn't a battery. It's the data pack."

"Huh. Interesting." He had more to say, but the door to the lower lab levels opened and a young blonde woman carrying a computer tablet came into the room, and she went right to him.

"What's that?" she asked, peering over the center island to get a look at it.

"A puzzle, it seems," he said, barely glancing at her. "Need something?"

She set the tablet on the island. "Latest test runs on the sub-micro nanobot chains. Drew needs them by Friday."

"I'll get to it." He was fixated on the fragment, which seemed to annoy her.

"Still on for lunch?" she asked, ignoring the fact that Will was standing right there and had the greater share of Finn's attention.

"Lunch. Ah." Finn finally looked at her. "I think I'm busy. My boy has some things we need to do."

"Your boy."

"Hello, I'm Will," Will said. "The boy."

That flustered her. "I'm sorry, I thought you were—"

"Dead? Yes, I am."

Finn snorted. "She doesn't have clearance, Dash. But that was funny."

"You employ people without the security clearance to know about the portals?" Will asked when she was gone.

"She has to earn it. She's newish."

"She's also irritated with you for bailing on your lunch date."

Finn set the fragment down. "One of my current life goals is to irritate her out of this ridiculous crush she seems to have. She's seventy years younger than I am, son. I want to buy her ice cream and send her out to play, not...date."

"You're allowed to date, Dad."

"Doesn't mean I want to. Especially not someone young enough to be my great-granddaughter."

"Come on. How long has it been? You don't need to be alone."

"Since Jo left." He gestured to the table and told Will to sit, and then got them each a cup of coffee. "I know we were broken and she needed to go. I know I was relieved to not have that daily irritation wrapped around us both. But I still miss her terribly, and if I could go back and change anything? It's that old axiom. 'If I knew then what I know now.' There are so many things I would do differently. If I only could."

"Dad." Will chuckled softly. "You have access to all the time in the world."

"With personal rules about creating fixed points that I do not cross."

Those fixed points had become fluid and were shifting all the time now. Once Eli moved forward and then lived in more than one When, and all the visits back and forth with Oz and Drew and all the manipulations with time they made in order to spend time with their grandchildren, time became a knotted tangle, not a thin, straight line.

"She's gone," Finn said thinly.

"I am aware."

Will had been with Jo in the end. She'd gone with young Eli far enough into the future to minimize the pain of losing her anchor—once she and Finn realized their anger was bigger than the both of them, the connection that kept time from flicking at her frayed—and Will had been there to hold her as she drew her last breath. It was the hours leading up to that, the truths they shared and the closure he'd given her, that he hadn't wanted to change when we were home in bed with Aisha. Now he was trying to talk Finn into interfering with that.

"She still needs to have left you," Will guessed. "You needed that time apart. But if you can forgive her?"

"Of course, I've forgiven her. Especially after—well, the months without hope of seeing her again, yes, I let go. But I don't know if she ever forgave me."

"You visited often, she told me as much."

Finn nodded.

"Then visit again. Pick a day that has enough distance from the pain, go see her. Tell her you still love her and you miss her."

"But—"

"And then save her life, Dad. She didn't die because she had no anchor. She died because she was ill and misunderstood the symptoms. She assumed what she felt was because she was displaced in time."

I'd curled up next to her, my paws on her skin, listening to everything going on inside her. Her lungs were wet and her heart was broken—but not in a lost-love kind of way—and all of it could have been fixed if she'd earlier accepted that it wasn't time turning against her.

"Interfering goes against everything," he argued, though it sounded more like he was trying to convince himself. "I drove her away, William. I blamed her, and yet it was my fault. And because I know when she dies? I can't. I can't just run after her and pretend."

Will sat back in his chair and thought about it for a moment. "She was filled with regrets in the end, you know. She realized that if she'd been honest when I was young, if she'd taught me to control my abilities when I was a child, I would have grown up and likely found love, and she would have had grandchildren. She wanted to be a grandmother in the worst way. The idea that I could go home and make the mother still in my life a grandmother? There was light in her eyes when she said that."

"I imagine you heard a few confessions."

Tell him how old he's going to be. And how mean he gets. And how sad.

"I'm sure he already knows that, Wick. How old, in any case."

Finn nodded sadly. "I'll see the end of the world, I know."

At that, Will leaned forward again, tapping the table with his pointy finger. "But this time, it doesn't end. The Finn yet to be born will succeed. Your world is not ending."

The idea that he would live even longer made Finn feel worse.

"I've met that man," Will said. "He's odd and miserable and is so conflicted about the things he's lost that he's trying desperately to recreate a life he once lived, if only to correct the things he got wrong."

Finn would one day go on to be Liam Finnegan, author of the Emperor stories Finn told Will when he was a small boy. He was a cranky old man who went to desperate lengths to have his son back, sending people into the past with the hopes of getting enough of Will's DNA that he could clone the son he'd lost. Will explained it all to Finn: a sect of the Cult of the Emperor, one that was less a cult and more a horribly misguided family, had gone in search of Will's spit or blood or even his toothbrush. He explained about Jay's stepfather getting in their way, subverting their effort of creating Will's clone by providing them with his own DNA, something that would have been nice to know before Will was dragged into court to defend against a paternity suit. It all led to a lonely old man who wrote books about his dead son, a broken soul trying to bring his son back to life. He told Finn about his offer to Liam Finnegan: give me time, let me have a child of my own, and then I'll *consider* proving you with the DNA you need.

He hoped that by the time that happened, Very Old Finn would realize that he didn't need Will's clone. He just wanted to be a father again.

It took long enough that their coffee went cold, and neither noticed when the blonde stomped through on her way out to the lunch date she wasn't having with Finn.

"Don't become Liam Finnegan," Will said.

"You're not cooperating with him, are you?" Finn asked, horrified.

"I haven't made up my mind. And honestly, as of last night, I argued against interfering in Jo's timeline. But now I'm thinking, why the hell not? I'll still have those moments of closure with her, but instead of letting them simmer with a sense of regret and longing, why not turn them into something better? Why not go forward and find a moment when she can be saved?"

"Then do that," Finn said softly.

"I can save her life. Absolutely. But I can't win her back for you."

Finn shifted uneasily. "You have your parents, Will. Go through the portal, and there they are."

"I know. But that doesn't change the fact that *you* are my father, as well. You're not an abstract being in another loop of time. You are my father. You are the man from whom I took an entire case of beer last night. I don't think of you as Other When. When I come here, I'm visiting my father. And when I return, I'll be coming to see my child's grandfather."

Finn's head snapped up.

"Tell me that baby will be another man's grandchild and not yours."

Finn pushed away from the table and got up so that he could put his arms around Will and kiss him. He stood like that for a long time, his head nestled against Will's, until Will leaned back and said, "I love you. In any When, I love you. And you're about to become a grandfather."

Another kiss and Finn let go of him. "Let's get your puzzle solved, Dash. We'll figure out what happened, and then we're finding a point in time to save your mother's life. She may not want to come home, but I am not robbing her of having a grandchild."

*

Instead of having lunch with the ticked off blonde, we had lunch with old Drew. I'd hoped we could see Jax and Aubrey, too, but they were lounging on a beach in Hawaii, guests of Bree Munson for the grand opening of her newest resort and hotel. Oz was tied up in a meeting and Zed was on Elysium, and we were lucky that Drew was available.

"I was supposed to go with Zed," he explained over pizza. "He's overseeing the memorial for one of Elysium's first caretakers. No family, few friends. I'd met the man a few times, and Zed wanted to be sure someone was at his service."

"Did the boys go instead?" Finn asked.

Drew nodded. "The boys and their wives, and Aubrey's younger brother, Hyrum. That filled the shuttle, and sadly, no room for me."

"You look broken up about that," Finn snorted.

Drew enjoyed Elysium when he was there for fun. He'd attended several memorial services at Zed's request, but the older he got, the harder those were. Each time reminded him that the day would come when Zed or one of his kids would lead a memorial for him, and he couldn't help picturing Oz in his head, broken by grief.

"I mean, she might throw a party. Who knows? But I'm starting to hate those services, knowing it's coming."

"You're young still," Will said. "Stop thinking about it."

"Tell me when I die, and I will."

"Not a chance. Your life span is not dictated by my history."

"Fine. Not that I won't keep asking. What's the deal, then? Something's up."

Will showed him the fragment and explained what we'd done. "We found this near the Ghirardelli factory in nineteen-hundred-six. There were dozens of pieces, but this was the largest. Molecular dating suggests it was manufactured here, but the technology is a hybrid of now and a hundred fifty years from now."

"Looks like one of mine," Drew said as he examined it. "Yet, it can't be. I can account for all the machines we built." He looked up. "What else did you find there?"

"Wick."

The color drained from Drew's face. "Oh god, no. Emperor, every animal we sent was a pregnant female, and every one of them came back. We never sent the offspring. By that point, Jo only wanted to know if the gifts the offspring were born with would continue in subsequent generations. And they didn't."

"What happened to the animals?"

The smallest of their test subjects—mice and hamsters and a guinea pig named Herculena—lived out their lives in the Ozoo Enterprise offices. They were office pets and well cared for. Most of the larger animals—small dogs and cats—were adopted. Employees were offered the first chance at providing forever homes for them, and many of them were taken in pairs, with one woman adopting two dogs and three of the cats.

A few of the cats became office pets, and some were sneaky enough to evade capture on days the veterinarian visited, so there were subsequent generations, all office pets. Rooms were set aside for them, large spaces with plush beds and climbing trees, and hutches with litter boxes. There was always food available, and each room had a tiny fountain to make sure there was always fresh water.

The office pets were spoiled, and he was proud of that.

"Overall, I think we sent six of the larger animals into null space. The size of their litters ranged from two to eight. Aside from the risks associated with their fear of being placed into the ships, we never subjected any of them to danger, Emperor. We made sure that they led happy lives and that they were well loved."

"Yet still. You engaged in animal testing."

"I know. It was the only way for Jo to get the answers she needed."

That made Will twitch, and Finn could feel his irritation building. "She needed the answers in a visceral way, Dash. It wasn't a whim. It was the only way for her to hang onto sanity at that point. Drew did it to keep her from—"

"I did it, that's all that matters," Drew said. "Judge me all you want, but I would do it again. I won't justify it to anyone, not even you."

"You're getting snippy in your old age, aren't you?" Will sighed, and let it go. "I only need to know about the ship this fragment came from. Are you sure every one of yours can be accounted for? No one else could have taken it when you were done with the initial testing?"

"Jo and I were the only ones involved in the launch phase. I've never given anyone else access to the testing and storage facility."

"You don't know for sure that Wick had anything to do with their project," Finn said. "Don't put the cart before the horse. It's not outside the realm of possible that someone else was working with similar technology."

Sure, someone else was popping kitties into the ether.

"What about DNA?" Will asked. "Did you keep samples of your subjects?"

Drew nodded. "I kept everything, Emperor. Every shred of data, every image we obtained from them. Internal scans, photographs, all of it."

"Will you allow me access to it?"

"I'll not only allow it, I'll help sift through it." He reached across the table and scratched between my ears. "Wick, if I did this to you, I am so sorry."

I was going to pee on you, you know. If you did it on purpose.

"No peeing on Drew. It was not intentional, if you were indeed part of the project."

Fine. Can I have some cheese from your pizza? I've been pretty freaking patient, you know.

He did know. I got the cheese, and some sausage to boot. After that, we were going to Drew's office, where I hoped I would find out where I began.

*

"All right," Will said as Drew pulled away from the curb, "be honest. How old were you before you caved in and learned to drive?"

Drew said, "Not old," at the same time Finn cackled, "He was thirty!"

"I didn't need to drive! Oz drove us around until my mother abdicated, and after that, I had a driver. What was the point?"

"I left you my car, didn't I?"

"Yes, but—"

"*That* was the point! So that you'd finally learn to drive!"

"Oz appreciated your car. Well, I did, too, even if I wasn't the one driving. I'm pretty sure Eli was conceived in the back seat."

Ew. Now you have to give it to them so that they have him.

"I think I can simply lend it to them."

With instructions? Like, park at Ocean Beach,

flip the seat down, don't get arrested, and bounce around until a baby pops out?

"I'll let them figure it out for themselves, Wick. I don't think I'll be consulted when they decide to start a family."

Finn reached over the back of the seat and hit Will on his arm. "Tell Drew!"

"I know how babies are made, Finn," Drew sighed.

"Apparently, so do I," Will said. "Aisha is pregnant."

"Hot damn." He grinned, and it was as big a smile as I'd ever seen on this older version of him. "That's amazing. I'm happy for you, Emperor. Even happier that when your Oz and Drew have Eli, you'll be used to the sleep deprivation when they shove him on you. They're going to want a break when he's three. And four."

"And five," Finn snorted.

"Ah, I'm looking forward to it. Remind me, Dad. Does Eli know who you are?"

"He's worked it out."

"But his wife doesn't know," Drew said. "And Eli was never told how old Finn is, nor when he was due to arrive. We've been intentionally vague about ages, and he's content to keep it that way. Or was. It depends on when we see him."

"Good for him. Let life come to him." He leaned forward to see out the window better. "Where are we headed?"

"The Presidio. Our offices take up a long stretch of Mason Street. Research and manufacturing take up a healthy portion of the rest of it." He glanced at Will. "We maintained the woods. None of the things you and Jax fought for have been torn down. Oz made sure that part of the land forfeiture agreements ensured that as long as San Francisco stands, so do the nature preserves within the city."

"They'll be there when I'm a boy, as well," Will said. "I spent many hours there."

"Hiding," Finn grunted. "I can't remember how many times I had people searching the woods for him."

"I would have come home on my own, Dad. Did you really think I would run away, all the way to Land's End? Five whole miles? Though I suppose I could have taken up residence in the Cliff House."

"Eh. Who knows. All I can be sure of is that I had enough panic over your absences to age me an extra decade or two." He tugged on a few strands of hair. "Look at this. This gray is all on you."

"Yeah, nothing to do with you being older than dirt," Drew said.

Finn sat back in his seat and pretended to pout. "You're not my favorite grandpa right now."

"Right now, I'm your only grandpa. Show some respect."

Is someone getting grounded? That would be awesome.

Ozoo Enterprises was a subtle entity, built to blend in with the surroundings. Drew's office building was only two stories high because anything more would have obstructed views from the structure behind it, and all of it was designed to reflect the natural structures in the Presidio. It curved along the street, with Crissy Field as its front yard. There were few people on the beach, and I could hear a small dog yapping its tiny head off as we got out of the car.

That thing is staying over there, right?

Drew led us into the foyer, where he signed us in. One by one—I had to walk through the metal and chemical detector by myself—we were scanned for contraband, and only when the security guards allowed it were we able to see the lobby. It was grand like the Westin hotel, where Oz and Drew had their wedding reception, but it was brighter and smelled more like cinnamon than floor cleaner.

We went down a long, brightly lit hallway with polished marble floors, and when we got to the end of it there was another security guard with another scanner, and again we each had to pass through it before we could move on. Finn went ahead of me and then turned to kneel, asking me to follow him as if I were a puppy in training. Normally that would have offended me, but I realized he did it for the sake of the guard, who didn't need to know I possibly had a larger vocabulary than he did.

We went through a door that led into a shorter hallway with a locked vault and Drew waited for the guard to secure the door behind us before he opened the vault.

"This is where Jo and I did a lot of our work," he said. "The security remains because of the sensitivity of the machines. She worried that anyone with easy access would ruin Finn's future research."

"You're using an incredible amount of old tech to protect valuable new tech," Will observed.

"We use visible means, Emperor," Drew said. "Old tech up front doesn't mean the entire campus lacks the best security available. Guards and sensors at entry points are only meant to remind people that we've taken tight control over everything."

Someone sneaking past a guard would get his asterisk lasered off the face of the planet.

He didn't say that, exactly, but I knew it's what he meant.

Lights popped on as we moved into the workspace. It was easily five times the space Will had at home, but there were no windows for me to look out, and there wasn't a dojo upstairs where Oz tossed Zed and Jay around. It felt cold and lonely, a place I had a hard time imagining Drew willingly spending much time.

There was a locked display case along the side wall, loaded with white egg-shaped machines in varying sizes. Will set me on a long, narrow lab table while Drew opened the first one, partially blocking my view, trying to spare me a sight that would frighten me.

I felt my skin begin to twitch and I shivered even though I wasn't cold.

"Most of these are nonfunctioning prototypes," he told Will. "These are the smaller units. The larger ones are back there." He gestured to a wide metal door at the far end of the room. "Jo spent a lot of time teaching me the basics of how they worked, and how to put all the pieces together. Initially, all we did was build, and she'd tell me what I was doing wrong."

"Sounds like her," Finn chuckled.

Drew plucked one off the shelf and turned around.

No. Put it back.

"Whatcha say, Wick. Want to test it for size?"

No no no no no no no no.

Make him put it back, Will.

I don't want to see it.

Put it back!

Please put it back.

"He's putting it away," Will said, nudging Drew to return it to the case. "No one is putting you inside one, I promise."

It's not fair. It wasn't fair. There was no room to move inside it, and there was all this noise. The noise was like tiny swords going into my ears and it never stopped. My head hurt, and I didn't have the words to tell him to let me out.

Don't make me do it again. I don't want to see the inside again.

"Never," Will breathed. "I swear."

I'm sorry. I'm really sorry. I didn't mean to.

"Wick, you didn't do—" He stopped when he saw what I'd done. "It's all right. I should have warned Drew that you have an aversion to the ships."

I peed on the table, Will. I'm sorry.

"That's my fault. I didn't give you a chance to go when we were outside. I'll get you cleaned up."

Drew went to another cabinet and pulled out a roll of disposable towels and a bottle of spray cleaner and told Will he would take care of it. He pointed to the nearby restroom and suggested Will clean me up in there, and as we passed, he apologized to me.

"Drew didn't know," Will said quietly as he wet a towel. "He would never have said that if he had."

I know.

"Your heart is racing. What did you remember?"

Drew wasn't there. I was in a big room and I tried to run because I was scared, then someone put me in the ship, but it wasn't Drew.

"Anything else?"

No. I'm sorry.

He set me on the bathroom counter and bent over to look me in the eyes. "None of this is your fault. You have nothing to apologize for."

But I peed.

"A little urine on the table won't hurt anyone. Besides, Drew has children. This isn't the first time he's cleaned up after someone. And I meant it, Wick, I should have given you the chance to go before we came inside."

You're going to use that wet towel on me, aren't you?

"I already did." He stood up and tossed it into a bin near the sink. "While you were talking, I was cleaning. It's just water. It will dry soon."

I didn't notice.

"That was the point. I know you don't like water on your fur."

Thank you. I'll walk out so your arms don't get wet.

"Wick." He picked me up. "Do you know how many times Zed peed on me? Or Oz? And Drew once peed in my hair. Your wet backside is not a big deal."

But it is.

He kissed the top of my head. "I'm sorry. I know it matters to you. But I promise, neither of them will think twice about it. I hope you're not embarrassed."

I am, a little. But I'll get over it.

Finn and Drew were examining the stored machines when we got back to them. They were all accounted for, and none were currently functional. There was a data bank to poke through, so Drew opened the door to the break room near the bathroom, and then brought three computer tablets in.

"I'll pull up everything we worked on. Between the three of us, maybe we can find something I just don't remember."

Good thing I peed already. This could take a while.

The break room had a sofa and three comfy chairs. Finn took the sofa, which was a mistake because three hours later Will looked up and laughed; Finn was asleep and had slowly listed to the right, until he was only half on the sofa with his legs dangling over the side. The tablet he'd been reading on dangled from his fingers and was more off his lap than on, so Will quietly got up and slid it out from under Finn's hand and set it aside.

"This might be a good time to take a break," Will told Drew. "I need to take Wick somewhere to get food, and I'm sure he needs to relieve himself again."

Just open the bathroom door for me and go back later to clean it up. I'll try to aim better than usual.

That was fine, but he was also sure I needed to eat and drink something, and he was hungry, too. Drew pointed to a small monitor fixed to the wall on the other side of the room and said we could order from there unless we wanted to wake Finn and go out. Ozoo Enterprises was a pet-friendly campus, and there were several choices of cat food available, and they could get anything from sandwiches to steaks for themselves.

"Does one of us need to go wait by the security guard for delivery?"

Drew pointed to a large port near the refrigerator. "Hover tunnels directly from the kitchen. What floats your boat, Wick? You can have anything from chicken to tuna to shrimp. Not even canned. The chef prepares the pet food himself."

We need this at home.

Will woke Finn when the food arrived—he swore he wasn't asleep, just resting his eyes, and what the hell happened to the tablet he was reading on—and we moved to the corner table. I had a plate with neat little piles of multicolored mush that tasted like happiness and joy, and they had grilled chicken and vegetables, which Drew didn't seem to want but he ate it anyway.

"Still not a fan of meat?" Will asked.

"You know that about me? I rarely eat meat. Honestly, if not for trying to feed four kids and making sure they ate well, I'd stop altogether. Oz already knows that once Sam is on her own, my carnivorous days are over."

"Synthetic proteins," Finn said. "They'd have done just fine."

"Yeah, well, tell Aubrey that. We were not putting what she considers to be fake food in our kids, not as long as she had control over the kitchen."

That made Will laugh. "She kept control for a long time, didn't she?"

"Aubrey had retired from teaching and Oz had stepped down from the throne before that happened. The boys were grown. Even after she and Jax moved upstairs, she wandered in every afternoon to cook for the family. We were not consulted about it, either. Either she was cooking in our kitchen, or we were all going upstairs for dinner."

"Like you minded," Finn said.

"We really didn't. Not having to consider how

we would manage meals for the kids was one less thing to worry about. They had the benefit of family dinners, and we didn't have to obsess over which one of us would work our schedules around it. Those dinners were such a gift."

"How did that work when you were King?" Will asked. "I know you and Oz juggled both countries, but where was Midlam's government seat after the war?"

"Still in Chicago. We went back and forth regularly, until we merged governments."

"And Aubrey went with them," Finn snorted.

"She did not. Not always."

"Only when you took the kids," Finn allowed. "When the kids stayed home, and Jax and Aubrey were traveling, it was Jo doing the hovering."

"And don't think we didn't appreciate that," Drew said. He told Will, "That was how she and Eli became so close. He took it upon himself to be her helper. He made sure his sister ate her vegetables, got a bath, and he read bedtime stories to her. When the other boys were in bed, he and Jo cuddled together on the sofa and talked until he fell asleep. She connected with all the kids, but there was something special happening with Eli."

"She got her grandchild after all," Will mused.

"She's why he went into medicine," Drew said. "And now he misses her horribly."

"As one would," Will said. "How old were you when she began this research?"

"Twenty-four? Twenty-five? Somewhere around then. I'd just started the company and opened the first of the buildings here. She leased space to play around with a few of her ideas while I worked on nanotech."

She hadn't wanted to set up in Finn's lab, surrounded by his technicians and interns. He had limited space for his own projects, and this was one she wanted to keep for herself. She hadn't told him exactly what she was doing, and Drew backed her up when she said she was only helping him get started in his own venture. Finn was focused on fine-tuning his transporter and didn't mind that she was working on something else.

"I think we all hoped that having something to concentrate on would help her power through her grief," Drew said. "I wish it had."

Shortly after launching the company, Drew became King of Midlam and his attention was divided among so many things that he didn't notice her increasing obsession with understanding what had happened to Will, and he didn't associate her project to grief that was swallowing her whole. Finn hadn't noticed, either, but by then the connection between them had become thin and frayed. He wasn't sure he wanted to notice that she was drowning in missing her son and the guilt she felt over never having told him what his potential was.

"And to this—" Finn reached for the tablet he'd been reading from "—I have her notes. Nothing in them makes me think she launched anything into null space other than the first generation of test subjects."

Drew took the tablet from him. "These notes end with the delivery of offspring from that first group. There should be data on breeding the second generation."

"I have data on the characteristic traits of the second generation," Will said. "I was hoping to find a cat that resembled Wick, but so far the advanced traits are limited to the first generation and fall along the lines of problem-solving abilities. Oddly, one with a demonstrative sense of basic math."

"Einstein," Drew said. "You could put objects in front of him and tell him to group them by number or to push a specific number away from a grouping. We eventually determined that he could handle addition and subtraction."

"Did he have verbal skills?"

"If he did, none of us had the ability to understand him. Any of those animals could have had that ability, Emperor. We had no way test for it."

They needed you for that.

Will scrolled through more of the data on his tablet. "Some of these notes are Jo's, some are yours, until approximately nine months into the project, when they're only hers."

"We had a baby. Well, Oz and I, not Jo and I. My time became even more limited."

"And shortly after that, she became Queen."

"We were busy for a very long time," he said. "I still managed to help Jo out some."

Will held the tablet out to him. "After the third generation, she locked the files."

"What?" Drew scowled as he looked at the tablet. "After the third, we began adopting out the animals. There was no fourth, other than the horny little office pets that evaded neutering."

"She was working on something. Otherwise, why encrypt the file?"

"Personal stuff?" Drew guessed. "She could have kept a journal here after we were done with the project. She had her answers, but she was still conflicted."

Finn took the tablet, reasoning that he knew most of the codes she'd used over time. Unless she'd set it to lock the entire tablet if a wrong code was entered, he might be able to get into the files.

While he worked, Will and Drew started clearing the table. It was such a normal thing for them to do but it almost broke my brain a little, because I kept tripping up over the idea that Drew was older than Will, and that's not how it was supposed to be. Drew was supposed to be twenty-one and still giggling over the idea that he slept in Oz's bed every night and no one cared; he wasn't supposed to look like Will's boss.

How'd he start this company? You're doing it together now. How'd he do it on his own?

"The Emperor invested heavily in it," Drew replied to Will's abbreviated question. He didn't tell Drew that they were starting it in our own When, years before he got around to it in this one. "You left us each a hell of a lot of money, Emperor. I think we all sat on and invested it for years before deciding how we wanted to use it to make a difference."

"My intention was to give you better lives. I hope it did."

"Oz and I started the company, and Zed purchased most of Treasure Island. We all began charitable foundations in your name. Your money managed to give a wide range of people better lives. Most still benefit from it."

Enjoy it because the next you isn't getting it.

"I think the next me would rather have the Emperor. And more free time. I have a few regrets about the amount of time I've spent on this place. Projects that seemed urgent enough to keep me away from home in hindsight were nothing more than giant time-sucking dead ends."

"I harp on you to make time with Oz," Will told him, "yet you're still stretching yourself rather thin between school and work."

Drew slid the washed-off plates back into the hover tunnel. "I'm working? How'd I manage that? Oz and I took a lot of crap from friends because we were supported by the state all through school."

"Midlam is no more," Will reminded him. "You lost your royal entitlements when Pacifica took over. You have a tuition fund, one that will carry you through to a postgraduate degree if you choose to go that far, and you have housing with the King, but you felt that you needed an income."

"That would have been nice. I wanted to work but was outvoted by a stubborn father-in-law who wanted me to earn a degree."

"He still does."

"Good for me. What kind of job does a former

prince land, anyway? Please tell me I'm busing tables at Fuzzy's. I wanted to do that so badly."

"Not quite so pedestrian an endeavor." If he was going to tell Drew more, Finn stopped him. He'd gotten into Jo's files but didn't think they would like it.

"There's a separate set of experiments, done fifteen years down the line." He sighed heavily. "You're going to be so angry, Drew."

"I'm not happy that she kept me out of it," Drew said, "but it was her project. She had the right to finish it the way she saw fit."

"He's right," Will grumbled. "You'll be upset. Her assistant?"

Drew took the tablet from him.

"Eli."

11

We waited on Union Square while Drew went home to get a phone that would work in Eli's future When. They'd debated about which When to go to on the drive back: drop in on the dates when Jo began the second set of launches or go after the fact and just get the data. Drew argued that it was necessary to stop her; she had the information she needed, she'd learned what she needed. Further testing was unnecessary and cruel. Finn thought that if they wanted to go there, he needed to stay behind because they were choosing a time when she was most angry with him, and most hurt.

"If I'm there, she might not see you, much less cooperate," he said.

And it would break his heart. I'm getting that about you people.

"Indeed, Wick," Will said under his breath.

Go after. If you stop her, I might not exist. Or I'll exist, but I won't find you and I might live my life in a lab's cage.

"A life in a cage is not what I want for you," Will said. "We'll go after. The end goal is not to stop her, but to discover Wick's beginnings. That's all."

When Drew went home, Finn had second thoughts. He'd visited her often, but it was usually tense. He loved her—that had never changed—but he'd always had a difficult time getting past the truths she'd withheld from Will and his visits usually devolved into arguments that neither of them could win. If she'd been honest, not just with Will but with him as well, their lives would have been different. Better. Will would have been happier.

"Happier in the moment," Will said. "But in the scope of my life? I'm not sure what it would have done for the son you lost, but those omissions made it possible for the life I have now. I'm truly sorry for the pain you went through, Dad. If I had lived, if your Will had lived, he'd be genuinely glad for it."

"I know." He leaned into Will, shoulders touching. "What do I say to her, Dash? I can't ask her to come back with me, not without an anchor."

"You have no anchor," Will pointed out.

"I'm an anomaly. Time is punishing me for my hubris."

Null space did this to us. It's made us live longer than we should. But I don't think it's punishing anyone.

"I've seen people die from lack of an anchor, Wick," Finn said.

That's not punishing. Time is like a dog, and people are fleas. When you hop around and nibble, you make him itch, and he scratches, that's all. Anchors keep you from nipping and wiggling around too much. So he doesn't scratch as hard.

"Then why doesn't time scratch at you and Dad?" Will asked.

Null space stripped us of the things that itch.

Maybe if everyone stops biting the dog, it'll leave them alone.

*

After we popped out of the portal onto Union Square, Drew steered us away from Finn's lab. It was still there, and undoubtedly so was the other, older version of Finn, and Drew didn't want to complicate things by piquing the intrigue of the significantly crankier Dr. Blackshear. That Finn would find little value in their interest regarding my When; it had happened, it was done, leave it alone. Whatever Jo was interested in, they were done.

We'd met him when he was even older, a grumpy old man still alive in Will's birth When. He left physics to pursue the study of genetics and cloning and had developed a tunnel-vision goal of bringing his son back to life. He'd gone so far as to send people after Will to steal his DNA; it was a hiccup in the road of Will's calm, gentle married life, but once he understood the reasons, he agreed to consider voluntarily giving Finnegan a sample of his DNA.

No one else thought he should do it, but he said he was still thinking about it.

Once we were a few blocks away, Drew called Jo to let her know he was coming. It wasn't an optional visit; he needed to see her, without Eli. He didn't mention Will—this Jo had no idea he'd survived—and he especially didn't tell her that Finn was along for the ride.

Without saying so, they all knew it would take time to get from seeing Will to being able to tell her why we were there. She would assume, as everyone did, that she was seeing him in the last days of his life. There would be a sadness mixed in with the joy, until he mentioned his age, then there would be disbelief.

He'd gone through it often enough to know that he had to allow people time to take it in. He'd already told her once, when she was older and dying, and he had told Eli, when he was not as young and was caring for her on that last day.

This version of Jo was in between. This Eli was younger and newly married, and Finn had not yet been born. The older Finn, the one who would see his 300th birthday in his 700th year, would leave the lab within a decade because it needed to be there for his future self. It was complicated, but Will kept it all straight in his head: he was about to see his mother in a moment when her grief was still heavy enough to have severed the connection between her and his father, and he was about to simultaneously break her heart again and relieve her of some of the pain.

Drew signaled a driverless cab and directed it to an address in the Marina district. Jo lived in a house that overlooked Marina Green and the bay, only a mile or two from Ozoo Enterprises. There was a courtyard bordered by tall stone walls and Drew entered a passcode near the heavy iron gate to gain access to the house inside. A few seconds later, the gate buzzed, and he led the way into the courtyard, which was populated by a dozen or more cats that really should have been warned that I was visiting.

The spitting and growling caused me to dig my claws into Will's shoulder, but I refused to dignify their reaction to me with a hissing fit of my own. I held onto Will, and we followed Drew and Finn up the stairs and into the house. Drew didn't bother knocking on the door; he went in as if it were home, and it was clearly familiar to him.

"She'll be in the study," he said as he closed the door and silenced the noise from the garden. "Finn and I should go in first—"

"The order in which we enter won't matter," Will said. "She'll see me behind you, and you'll cease to exist for ten seconds."

Drew gestured for Will to go first, pointing out the study's door, and they fell into step behind him. I think Will expected her to be sitting quietly, old and in pain, the way he'd seen her on her last day, but this Jo was on a ladder shelving books, and she didn't look down when she heard us come in.

"Just give me half a second, Andrew," she said. "I need to put this out of Luxor's way. The big brute has taken to chewing on things, and these books are too valuable to let that old fleabag near. They were Wi—"

"Luxor," Will repeated. "Feline or canine?"

She froze in place for a moment and then turned. There was the fleeting sadness he expected, but then she broke out with a wide grin and slid down the ladder, as spry in her nineties as she'd been in her thirties. "Oh my god, William, you're alive!"

"I believe so, yes."

"I knew it. I knew that one day Finn would figure it out stop the damned meteor." Her feet hit the floor and she ran over to him, throwing herself into his arms. "And you brought Wick!"

"You really are something else," he said as he pressed a kiss to her head. "Everyone always thinks I'm about to die. You knew. How?"

She took a step back and placed her hands on his cheeks. "The William who died would never come forward. I always knew that if I saw you again, it would be because Finn found a way, Wick never died, and you felt free enough to come."

Finn looked at Drew and said, "See? I'm a hero."

"I'll give you credit," Jo said. She let go of Will and leaned over to kiss Finn. She kissed him on the lips, too, which made his eyes go wide and made Drew snort. I was about to make fun of him, but then she snatched me off Will's shoulder and squeezed me, which would have been unfortunate if I hadn't peed before we left Drew's offices. "I've missed you, Major Wick."

You didn't answer Will. Is there a giant dog running around here who might want to eat me?

Luxor was a long, thin, tall, brilliantly white cat with piercing bright blue eyes. He strolled into the study as she was handing me back to Will, and he came up to rub against her leg, purring. He noticed me but didn't seem to care that I was there, nor that his human had just shown me a lot of affection.

Sorry, dude. It's just that she knew me when I was a kitten and she missed me.

Luxor sat down and stared up at me. *'I know who you are. You're the cat who came before me. The one that mattered, anyway.'*

Will, can you understand him?

"No, Wick, I'm sorry. I don't."

'No human does. And you're the first cat who has. I'm intrigued.'

I asked Will to set me on the floor so that Luxor didn't have to look up at me. We sniffed each other's noses, just to be polite, and I was relieved when that's all he wanted to sniff.

He cocked his head and said, *'You're very small for a cat so old. If I didn't know better, I would think you belonged with the kittens.'*

I'm holding up well.

'Still, you're quite young for one so ancient.'

I was surprised that he had any sense of my age, but he could feel time rolling off me, and guessed that I'd lived for centuries. When the people sat down to discuss Will's life and why we were there, Luxor offered to show me where the food was—*'She always leaves plates full, in case a hungry outsider wanders in'* —and we had a snack before he gave me a tour of Jo's home.

Zed would think it was wasted space, a house big enough for more than one family but lived in by only one person. Aubrey would love all the tiny details, from the polished fake marble floors to the intricate elements carved onto the stair banister. I thought it was the perfect place for a cat, with more room to chase the red dot than I could ever hope for and dozens of napping spots.

'Before Eli married, he lived here. He may live here again. Jo says they're always welcome, as long as they don't chase away the cats.'

How many are there?

'I've lost count. New ones come, and she feeds them. Old ones leave but return when hunting is lean.'

The neighbors must love her.

'There was one who didn't, but he left a long time ago. The other neighbors help her clean up after them.'

How long have you been here?

'All of my days. I was born here, in a bedroom upstairs, from a cat who came here with Andrew. I was the only one of her litter to survive. Jo said I was meant to be hers.'

Your mom was one of the Ozoo kitties? We might be related.

'I would enjoy that, I think. The outsiders are company, but they're not family.'

I told him about Finn bringing me home—a story he'd heard but allowed me to tell nonetheless—and how tenderly Jo cared for me in those first weeks, bringing me back from the brink of starvation and certain death. That was why he had no desire to join the outsiders; she was gentle and kind, and her heart seemed to need him.

Maybe you're her anchor.

He feared that he was. She loved him and depended on him for companionship, but he knew his life was limited. *'My days will end soon. I don't know what will become of her.'*

You're not old, dude. You might have a dozen years left. Maybe more, because she takes awesome care of things.

'Listen.'

He laid on the floor and rolled over, exposing his belly, and invited me to touch him with the pads on my paw. I carefully set it on his chest, and we were quiet for a long time as I listened to his heart and his lungs, until I heard the soft wetness that was just beginning to form around his heart. One side beat bigger than the other, it took longer for the blood to move through.

You need to tell her. She can fix you.

'I don't have the words for her.'

Dude. I do. Will understands everything I say to him. Just tell me what you want Jo to know, and he'll pass it along.

He rolled back over and sat up, then rubbed his head against mine. *'Give the words gently. Her life has been painted with melancholy. I don't want her to be broken.'*

I was sure she wouldn't be; his wetness was new, there was time to fix him. We walked back to the study—I wanted to run but then realized I didn't want to pop his heart right after he found someone who could tell her what was wrong—and when we entered the study, she was sitting forward in her chair, elbows on knees, and she looked confused.

"I never sent another test subject, Drew," she said. "Yes, Eli and I built a few machines and launched them, but it was only to teach him a bit of the engineering necessary in everything we do. He had a brief interest in his father's work, and I tried to fan the flames. There were no live subjects, just a few dolls. He found the idea of using toys as pilots amusing."

Will. Will. Will.

"Just a minute, Wick."

Luxor stretched up on his back legs and nudged Jo to sit back so that he could take her lap while we waited.

Dude, you are the most chill cat I've ever known.

I crawled onto Will's legs and curled up. It could be a while. They were animated and excited, but still not any closer to knowing who had shot me out into null space and left me there.

"How old was Eli when you started this?" Drew asked.

"Fourteen, maybe fifteen. He was fascinated by the whole notion of null space and how we bounced ships off it. We built three ships together, and then he built one on his own. We launched a few, they came back, and he studied the data."

"Fifteen was a rough age for him," Drew mused. "He was sullen and quiet for most of that year. What happened?"

She had no idea. "Once he'd built his own ship, I think he tired of it. The process of creating something interested him, but he loathed combing through the data and trying to make sense of it. He grew tired of the repetition. I tried to explain that he needed more information and as his math and cognitive skills progressed so would his ability to fit the pieces together, but he didn't want to wait for that."

"Didn't he decide he was more interested in helping living things at that point?" Finn asked. "Seems to me that right around sixteen, he began leaning toward the biological sciences and Drew's work with surgical nanobots."

"The files Dad accessed were clearly entered under your name, Mom," Will said.

"But not by Eli," she said, her voice cracking. "He wouldn't."

"He might know who did," Finn said. "Let's get him over here and find out."

When Drew stepped out of the study to call his son, I poked Will with my paw and told him he needed to listen. I explained about Luxor's heart and how he hadn't been able to tell Jo what was happening, but it was new, and there was time.

"Is he certain, Wick?"

I listened to his insides. I can hear it. One side of his heart beats bigger than the other, and it's wet.

"Are you in pain?" he asked Luxor, which made Jo stiffen.

'Not yet. But soon.'

"He needs to see a vet, Mom," Will told her. "Luxor has issues with his heart but feels it's early enough that if he gets the proper care, he'll be all right."

'She's going to hug me now, isn't she?'

She did.

She scooped him up and held him tight and told him over and over that she was sorry she hadn't noticed. Then she looked at me and said, "Thank you, Wick. I can't imagine what he would have gone through."

I'm here to serve.

"I need to find you a better vet," she told Luxor. "Someone who will treat you the way you deserve. Not that bastard I took you to last year. He acted like you were nothing more than an animal."

"There's always Martinson," Finn said.

"I'm certain he's dead by now." She chuckled, even though it wasn't funny. "Don't worry, I'll find someone."

"Bring him home, JoJo."

Will excused himself. He set me on the chair while he pretended to go to the restroom, and I was pretty sure he was going to tell Drew to stay out for a while.

"Home," she repeated.

"A few years north of the home you left." He took a deep breath. "This feels odd because this is completely out of sequence and I've visited you here dozens of times after this date, but…"

She waited.

"I miss you. I've missed you from the day you left."

"You agreed it was necessary."

"We needed time, Jo. If I'd thought that there was a point when you would have come back—things have changed. I've changed. I've pulled my head out of my ass."

She raised an eyebrow.

"What? I showered."

She stroked Luxor's fur, staring down at him while she composed her thoughts. He leaned into her hand and forced her to scratch under his chin and was far pushier about it than I'd ever been.

I needed to remember that.

"How old are you now, Finn?" she finally asked. "We're so far out of synch."

"I know. And the years between us are mired in regret on my side. I imagine you're still angry with me, but I'm begging you, look past it." He sighed. "Yes, I'll beg. I'm older than you are now, but not by so much that it will matter."

They locked onto each other, and neither blinked until Luxor yawned, letting out a twisted meow when he did. That brought Jo out of it, and she laughed lightly. "Silly boy," she told him.

"Whether you do or not, hear this. I have always loved you, even when we were both broken beyond hope."

Oh, that was good.

'It was good,' Luxor agreed. *'Corny, but acceptable. I like him.'*

"I know that. I'm not hesitating because I don't love you. I need to know why, and why now?

Why not go find me at the age I would be if I'd stayed, and ask me then?"

"I've wasted my years. I don't want to waste yours."

Will quietly stepped back into the room, and they both turned to look at him. "Mom, If he waits, he loses you forever. He was willing to bear the pain when it was just himself, but you both have me now. I fully intend to continue visiting you."

She let that sink in. "He loses me forever. I'm going to die soon, then."

"Not now," Finn insisted. "Whatever else happens, I won't allow that. Come home or not, but I'll make sure you get help when you need it, and I refuse to hear you tell me no. Time isn't what comes for you, JoJo. And I—" His breath caught. "He held you while you died. I should have been there. No, you shouldn't have—"

"Dad."

"No, let me get this out. I let you leave thinking it was your fault, and we argued endlessly over it every time I visited. I pushed the point that you'd known since he was a toddler that he would eventually learn to control what happens when he touches people and you didn't tell me. You didn't tell him. But I never took responsibility for my own part in it, and I know, I *know* that it was more my fault than yours."

"Finnegan—"

He words poured out. He wasn't there; even when they were together his attention was divided, trying to think of innovative ideas about how they could push the meteor off its path. He was so absorbed in that, and in building the tunnel and opening the portals, that he didn't notice the shadow of unhappiness creeping up on her. They had a child together, and the free time he had, he spent with his son. He counted on her to raise him, educate him, play with him, and had shoved aside the reality that she needed a partner and not just a warm body on the other side of the bed.

"I know we connected," he said softly. "I think you knew how much I loved you. But I wasn't there the way I should have been, and when it comes down to it, I didn't have the right to question the decisions you made. Even if you'd tried to talk to me about it, I probably would have been distracted. I might have heard the words, but I wasn't listening."

"Finny."

"If nothing else, I need you to know that. It took me too long to reach down deep enough to understand my anger. Not until Will showed up to tell me he'd lived."

She smiled softly. "That's why you went to me on my last day, isn't it?"

Will nodded. "I wanted to leave you with some peace. But now there's no need. Dad's right, we're not letting you get that far."

"And he's coming back to visit," Finn said. "Often."

She sighed, in a happy way. "You have your parents, Will, I realize that."

"And their existence doesn't change the fact

that you are my mother. I hope you'll want to see me and to meet my wife—"

"Shut up!" She dropped Luxor to the floor and shot out of her seat. "You got married?"

"She's a wonderful woman," Finn said. "You'll adore her. She has a son I haven't met yet, too."

But wait, there's more!

"Wick, really," Will snorted. "But he's right, there's more. Don't ask me how I know, but I know—you've always wanted to be a grandmother."

In a rush of breath that belied the word, she said, "No."

"My life would be a lot less complicated if I only had one other When to bring my family when I visit. I know this is selfish, but if you go home with him, you'll see me often."

"Just visit," Finn pleaded. "Bring Luxor to see Martinson. We'll talk then. We'll have dinner."

"He's asking you on a date, Mom. Unless you have some hidden boy toy here?"

"William."

"Well, you're technically single."

"No, really, I'm not." She looked at Finn. "I don't know what's happened on your end, in the years in between now and then, but we're not divorced."

"We never divorced. I'm not seeing anyone," he said. "I haven't."

"Well, there's the blonde," Will teased. "Maybe you're not seeing her, but she wants you."

"You're not helping."

Jo sighed. "Will, there have been a dozen blondes over the years. He never notices when they're flirting with him. He always assumes they're just *really* excited about their jobs."

"No one flirts with me."

She started ticking off names, and with each one Finn's cheeks flushed a little brighter. "Cassandra Hopper. Remember her? We took the techs to dinner one night, and she slapped you on the ass and called you 'sugar.' You honestly thought she was just a little bit drunk and was only teasing you."

"He does seem to have a bit of attention deficit at times," Will said.

"Why would I have paid attention to anyone else?" Finn asked. "I had the love of my life right there, and everyone else paled..." He sucked in a deep breath, and then quietly added, "I'm sorry. That's not fair of me."

Drew came back, shoving the phone into his pocket. "He wasn't answering so I called Harper. He's out studying, and if we interrupt him she's going to find new and creative ways to hurt us."

Will tilted his head to look over the back of the chair. "Go away. My dad is trying to hit on my mom and is failing miserably. If you stay, he'll stop trying."

"Gross." Drew scrunched his nose up and dropped back into his chair. "Throw him a bone, Jo. Maybe he'll stop talking about you nonstop if you do."

"I do not," Finn grumbled. "Do I?"

"He came to dinner last week," Drew said. "He brought this *thing* that was supposed to be a cobbler, and said he'd made it because you would have loved it. But no, you would not have." He touched his fist to his chest. "I can still taste it."

'I'm going back with these people?' Luxor asked me.

I think so. By the time we're done here, those two are totally gonna kiss.

"We can come back," Will said. "Will Eli be available in the morning?"

"Nonsense," Jo said after Drew nodded. "You'll stay here tonight. There's plenty of room, and I wouldn't mind the company at dinner."

Great, she's making dinner for us, and we're all going to die here in the future.

'It's not just me, then?' Luxor asked. *'I don't have defective taste buds?'*

When Will was growing up, we had delivery services on speed dial for a reason.

Finn cooked; Jo knew better than to presume he offered out of graciousness. On the grand scale of cooking, there was Aubrey at the top, Aisha at the bottom, with Jo barely a slot ahead. We all would have been happier if Will cooked, but he understood it was something important for Finn. Cook for her, provide something, let her see that he wanted to make her happy, even if the result resembled a failed grade school science project.

Luxor and I watched from the top of his cat tree in the dining room—he had the same rule I did: be good, don't beg, and you get a bite—and then we ate while Will and Drew did the dishes. They lounged in the spacious living room after dinner and talked late into the night, until Jo told Luxor to show Will and Drew where the guest rooms were.

Finn stood when they did, uncertain about where he was expected to go. "Am I shacking up with my son or my grandfather?"

Jo cocked her head to the side just a touch, and said, "You're still my husband, Finn." She grabbed his hand and tugged him along, and as they headed for the stairs, she added, "If you want me to come home to a man older than he should be, then I want to see what I'm getting."

"No pressure, Dad," Will yelled up the stairs.

"Finn's a hundred years old." Drew scrunched his nose and grimaced. "I didn't need to hear that. God, I hope they're quiet."

*

At almost forty-four, Will still looked like he was in his early thirties. Eli was in his early twenties, and when he walked into Jo's study, it was like Will's little brother had come home from college for summer break. It caught Finn by surprise, seeing them in the same room, looking as if they belonged together. His hand went to his mouth for just a moment, and he uttered, "Oh, wow," and then chuckled as he added, "Those Blackshear genes are *strong*."

Eli paused at the entry; he was doing the

math, trying to figure out how old his father was. "We're a little off schedule here, aren't we?" he finally asked. "Six, seven years? More?"

Drew nodded. "A bit. Take notes, remember to not mention it to me later unless I bring it up."

"So, the usual." He came all the way in and grinned. "Emperor. You have no idea how badly I've wanted to meet you."

Will probably had an idea; Eli wanted to meet him as much as Will had wanted to meet the Emperor when he was a boy.

"You've met before, haven't you?" Drew asked.

"No," they said together.

"But last... Hm."

Eli laughed. "He may have met me. This is the first time I've met him."

Will didn't want him to examine that too closely. "And we'll leave it at that, all right? The next time won't happen now."

That piqued Eli's curiosity, but he knew better than to press for details. He dropped onto the sofa and patted his lap, asking Luxor to come over and say hello. I followed him over and jumped onto the seat next to Eli, sniffing at his arm.

"Hello. Who might you be?" he asked. "Another outsider decided to come in and stay?"

"That's Wick," Jo told him.

"No freaking way!" He held his fingers out for me to sniff, testing to see if I would let him pet me. I rubbed against him because he was Drew's son and that meant I liked him no matter what. "Is it true that you can converse with him, Emperor?"

"It's true."

"Amazing."

Yeah, you're Drew's kid, all right.

"Wick and Luxor understand each other!" Jo said brightly. Then just as quickly, the joy in that faded. "Both the upside and downside to that is that he was able to tell us that Lux is on the cusp of a serious medical issue. It's his heart."

Eli lifted him up. "I'm sorry, Lux. How bad is it?"

"Treatable if I get him seen soon," Jo said. "At least Lux thinks so."

'Please set me down. This is embarrassing.'

"God, don't take him back to that quack. We'll find him someone better, someone who doesn't think you're a crackpot for having all the cats and expecting human-level medical care for them."

Jo sighed and sat next to him, pulling me onto her lap. "About that. Finn wants me to take Luxor home, to see our old vet."

"Dr. Martinson? Well, he's certainly good with cats," Eli said, though he sounded uncertain. "He'd probably have to stay there for a while, depending on the level of care he needs. If there's surgery involved, there will be rehab—" He sighed. "You're going back to stay, aren't you?"

"I don't know. Finn and I are at different places in our lives, and I'd be returning over a decade after I left. But...we talked about it all night. We miss each other, horribly. So, we're going to give it a try and see how well we can live together again."

For the time it took to inhale, he was upset.

He'd left home to give her an anchor, understanding he would live his life in more than one When, but she was the one who was supposed to stay here. He had only planned on staying long enough to make sure time wasn't going to destroy her, but then he met Harper, and everything changed.

He wasn't leaving for good, no matter what, so by the time he exhaled, it passed.

"Well, I can visit you there, you can visit me here. It's not like life will be much different if you decide to stay there and shack up with my wrinkled old son."

"Hey." Finn crossed his arms. "That's mean."

"Aw, are your feelings hurt?" Eli snorted.

Finn turned to Will. "Next time he's born, be as mean to him as you were to Drew. Take away his toys and make him hide in the closet."

"Oh yeah," Drew chuckled. "I forgot about that. He used to growl at me."

"Because you were constantly throwing things at Oz. And before you protest, I realize she started it most of the time. I growled when you were older to keep you from acting on all those inappropriate thoughts running through your head."

"Me? Emperor, if anyone was thinking those thoughts, it was Oz. Once we decided—"

Eli stopped him. "Ugh, Dad, just…no."

"Oh, so you're fine with your wrinkled old son taking Jo home and doing unspeakable things to her, but not with your parents talking about it? That's where I was going, Eli. We talked about it, a lot."

"And Oz was the one doing most of the thinking," Will said lightly.

"Really, can we switch back to talking about Jo going home?"

'What about the outsiders?' Lux asked.

I relayed the question to Will, who reminded them that there was a colony of cats to consider.

"I'll take care of them, Emperor," Eli said. "They're not as much trouble as they might seem, and my wife loves them."

"If I stay there, you and Harper get the house," Jo told him. "And I'll understand if you thin the colony a bit. Find them good homes. I know I'm too soft."

"Kindness isn't the same as being soft." He let Luxor slide off his lap to sit on the coffee table. "I could learn a few more lessons about that."

"You're very kind—" Drew started to say.

"I wasn't fishing, Dad. And I know you're here for something else, not just to tell me Jo is going home." He leaned his shoulder against hers. "Where you probably belong. I know you missed him."

"He's older than me now, you know."

"Good. Maybe he's matured."

Will slid the tablet across the coffee table toward him. "We're trying to understand some of the data in Drew and Jo's null space projects. She thought you might have some insight."

He explained what we'd done and why, and after some time I realized Eli was staring down at the tablet, refusing to look at anyone. He scrolled absently through the files as if he were searching for the answer they wanted, not settling on anything. I wiggled off Jo's lap and pulled myself partway onto his leg and looked at him.

His face was flushed, his eyes moist and rimmed red.

Will noticed but said nothing. He carried on a conversation with Drew and Finn, musing about the things I'd likely gotten into during the years I was alone. He explained my upset over not being able to remember everything, but Finn said that was normal. He didn't think a human with a lifespan forty times longer than it should be would be able to retain all their memories, why would I expect to?

"It's nothing to do with intelligence," he said. "The brain is a storage device. Like any computer drive, there's only so much available to write the data on."

"Then the memories are there, but overwritten," Will said. "Data can be retrieved."

"If necessary. Wick may need to accept that he's written over the things he doesn't want to remember. Not every person or event is worth holding onto."

'He's saying your brain is tiny.'

Hey. I thought I liked you.

'I enjoy sarcasm. If I upset you, tell me. But I've never been able to use it on anyone before.'

Dude, you are totally going to fit in with the entire family. They pick on each other all the time.

'But not now. Eli is upset.'

I noticed. He's pretending to search the tablet.

I watched his fingers slide over the screen, scrolling up and down, pausing every now and then for effect. I saw every fold of the skin on his hand, the way his knuckles jutted and how the veins tugged as his fingers moved. There was a tiny scar near the base of his pointy finger and another on his little finger, and his middle finger bent to the left so minutely that one wouldn't notice unless they were looking for that sort of thing. He'd broken it somehow.

A punch thrown at someone's face.

Then another. And another.

Will set the fragment on the coffee table, expecting Eli to pick it up.

Stop. Just stop. Put it away. I don't need to know anymore.

"We've come this far, Wick," Will said. "We might as well see it to the end."

No. We're done. Jo's going home, and Finn gets to be happy and I don't need to know anything else. I don't have to remember my beginning. We need to leave it alone.

He sat forward in the chair, bending to look closely at me. "What did you just remember, Wick? What don't you want us to know?"

Eli finally set the tablet aside. "He's probably trying to protect me. What happened to Wick was my fault."

No. He didn't do it. I know he didn't do it.

"Then who did?" Will asked.

I don't know. But Eli didn't do it. He beat the snot out of the person who did. He tried to stop him, I swear.

"Eli?" Drew's voice was thick with dread. "Explain."

"Thatcher," Eli whispered.

Drew, Finn, and Jo all sagged in their seats, a collective groan uttered in both understanding and disbelief.

Only Will was confused, but he sat back and waited for the explanation.

It's not his fault. It was never his fault.

'I believe you,' Luxor said.

Make them listen, Will. Don't blame Eli.

12

Even though his interest in launching the ships they'd made together waned, Jo left Eli with unfettered access to her workspace. He was free to spend time digging through the files she hadn't encrypted, and she encouraged him to study the work she'd done with Drew. He also had free rein to roam the main office building of Ozoo Enterprises, and with that came access to the cats that roamed the hallways and cubicles.

These were animals that were smarter than average but had no unusual gifts that she could determine, and they were loved members of Ozoo. There was nothing curious about Eli's interest in them, and nothing suspicious about the time he often took to play with them, feed them, and clean up after them. He frequently came without being asked, for no reason other than he wanted to be sure someone regularly provided feather toys to chase, and that someone brushed them and cleaned all the little spaces in the rooms they were given as their own.

There was also nothing unusual about him bringing along a friend or two. He didn't have access to the buildings where research and testing were conducted and only minimal access to the lab where Drew was focused on evolving nanotech. He could observe through a window but was never given clearance to enter the room.

Other than the animals, that workspace held his interest the most; he'd spent long afternoons with Drew discussing the work he'd done to make Elysium a reality and holographic imaging a flourishing field, and together they mulled over what Drew hoped to achieve in medicine. He knew those tiny machines would become valuable surgical and treatment tools, but he had to make them smaller and more efficient.

Eli was torn between his interests. He considered Jo to be every bit as much his grandmother as was Aubrey and he desperately wanted to make her happy. He was genuinely interested when they built the small ships, knowing they were defying time by launching them into null space. The directional capabilities employed in the vessels were limited because they were pilotless, but he was able to watch as they disappeared on one end of the track and reappeared on the other.

He was fascinated by the bits of video each launch obtained. They were short bursts of bright light, snippets of purple-hued nothingness, and then a flash of stars before another burst of light, but it was proof enough—the ships he'd built had gone somewhere. They had touched time.

"I let my ego get the best of me," he explained. "I'd taken Thatcher to help clean out the cats' rooms and bragged about the ships I'd built with Jo. He didn't believe a word of it. While I cleaned the boxes in room seven, he sat in a chair mocking everything I'd claimed, and said he couldn't wait for school on Monday so he could tell everyone what a useless, lying moron I was. The pathetic Prince of Pacifica. The boy who would never be King because his mother was a quitter. I lost it. I told him I could prove it."

After the boxes were clean and fresh food set out, he picked up one of the small cats that had been born to one of the older felines, one who always hid when strangers entered the office, when he impulsively decided to take Thatcher into Jo's workshop. The small egg-shaped machines were lined up in a display case, and he pointed to the last in the line, one he'd built completely on his own. He plucked it out of the case and booted up the computer that controlled the track, and then rigged the machine to launch.

He handed the cat to Thatcher while he set the launch sequence in motion and felt vindicated when it sped down the track and disappeared just before it would have smashed into the wall. He told Thatcher to turn and watch the back wall, and a few seconds later it appeared with a pop and stopped to rest in front of them.

"He set the cat down to check out the ship, and I opened it to show him the inside. He almost believed me then. He wanted to run it through again, and I did, and he watched carefully how I did it. It was after that I made the biggest mistake—"

His breath caught.

"It would be easier to show you." He lifted the tablet and looked at Jo. "The security recordings are on here. If I could hook it up to your office system?"

She gave a slight nod and went over to the bookcases where she'd been shelving books when we arrived. There was a small disc the same color as the wood just behind a book that probably made Drew drool—I recognized the author name, Heinlein, his favorite—and she flipped the cover off the disc and leaned in close. When the system recognized her eye, there was a soft click, and both sides of the bookcase slid forward and then apart.

Her office was behind them. It was as ornate as the rest of the house, but the floor was dark and wooden, and instead of paintings she'd hung photographs. There were several large framed photos of Will at various ages, including some with Jax and Aubrey when he was barely 18.

In the middle of the back wall was a photo taken when he was 19, in the parklet where they often went after Jax's classes. Will's hands were shoved into his jeans' pockets, and he was grinning as Jax sat on the playground swing; standing nearby, leaning on the swing's frame and smiling at him was a very young Aisha.

He stopped in the center of the office and stared at it, a slow smile coming to him.

"Aubrey gave that to me," Jo told him. "She said the girl was the one who got away, the one you never got over. Was she?"

"The girl I chased away," he replied. "But, she's forgiven me. With any luck, I'll have nearly a hundred years to make it up to her."

"Will." His name escaped her like breath. "Your wife?"

"I can't wait for you to meet her."

"Do I approve?" she asked, teasing him.

"Honestly, you don't think I'm good enough for her."

Eli had his back to them. He'd gone straight for the giant monitor on the right side of the room and was sliding his tablet into a connection pod under the control console. Luxor and I jumped onto Jo's surprisingly tiny desk to watch; Drew and Finn pulled up chairs, but Jo and Will stuck to the center of the room. She'd slipped her arms around his waist for a quick hug, less concerned with what Eli was doing than how happy she was to have her son there.

'I don't believe I've ever seen her this giddy,' Lux said, his head cocked to the side as he considered her. *'Is this typical? I'm not familiar with the habits of human mothers and their offspring.'*

She hasn't seen him in a long time, and the last time she did he died. Her whole life just changed, dude. It got better.

'Good. And your life, if what Eli has to show you is horrible?'

I don't know, but if it's really bad I'll try to not pee all over the desk.

Once he had the tablet connected and found the file he wanted them to see, the image on the monitor split into six frames. We watched, silently, as a smaller, thinner Eli scrubbed a litterbox clean while a taller, beefier boy sat in a chair in the corner. While Eli worked, the other boy chattered, and the longer it went on, the more agitated Eli became.

We saw the flick of a tail too long to be mine in the upper right corner, and by the time he was setting the litterbox back into its nook, a kitten barely bigger than his fist jumped into the frame. He'd hardly glanced at it when he scooped it up and nuzzled it close; he was calming himself as much as he was the kitten, but the effect didn't last long.

There was no sound, but he was obviously upset and speaking loudly to the other boy. On his lips were the words he wished he could take back: "I'll prove it."

As they left the room, Eli pressed a button to change the video, and we watched them argue as they walked down the hallway to Jo's workspace. He still had the kitten in hand, gently stroking his back despite his anger.

There was no guard on duty, no one to prevent Eli from taking Thatcher past the security scanner and through the vault. He hammered the code onto the access panel with his middle finger, and when the door slipped open, present-day Eli pressed the button again and started playing the recording of the footage taken from four angles in the room. He watched long enough to see himself close the workshop door, and then turned away, moving to the back of the room, where no one would be watching him.

His face was pinched with shame; he glanced at Drew, who stared at the monitor, silently, his own jaw set.

I felt the shame and the anger roll off them.

I remembered.

Turn it off. We don't need to know.

Will glanced over his shoulder. "I think by this point we do, Wick."

Drew got out of his chair and went to the control console, poking at the keyboard before sitting back down. He'd closed all the frames but one, and with that came sound.

"Don't touch anything," young Eli said to Thatcher. "This stuff is built with wicked precision and knocking anything even a hair out of alignment will screw it up."

"Yeah, wouldn't want to hose up your fairy tale."

Eli set me in the crook of his arm and went to the display case, pointing at the ship he'd built. "This one's mine. Jo let me do everything, from casting the metal and carbon fiber, to designing the interior. I even gave it a view screen like the big ones."

"For what?"

Eli chuckled. "She let me put action figures in the pilot space. I figured if there was a pilot, there needed to be a view screen. It was stupid, but I thought it was funny." He pulled the door open and lifted the small ship from its display stand,

and then took it to the track where he set it onto the docking port. They were quiet as he booted up the computer, and when the track hummed to life Thatcher twitched, as if he finally expected something decent to happen.

Eli needed both hands to type the launch sequence, so he handed me to Thatcher. I watched Eli's fingers fly over the keyboard; I remembered seeing it up close, wanting to jump over to him, to chase a finger or two, but Thatcher had a good enough grip on me that I wasn't going anywhere.

Within seconds, the ship shot forward, vanishing just millimeters from the wall.

"Turn around, watch the back wall," Eli told him. "In three, two, one..."

With a pop and a flash, the ship sailed down the track and stopped in the same spot it had started from. Thatcher was finally fully engaged; he set me down and went to the ship, his mouth hanging open when Eli pressed three fingers to the ship's hull and opened it. "The engine is in the back, it's that red cluster of blocks. The fuel is pulled from plasma batteries fused to the hull all the way around."

"What's this?" Thatcher asked, pointing to the front end.

"Control panel. I mean, if this carried a person, that's what it would be."

"Do it again."

Eli closed the door and went back to the computer, ignoring that Thatcher stood so close that he could feel breath brushing against his cheek. They both laughed when the ship vanished and reappeared, though Thatcher argued that it didn't prove anything about time travel.

"You might have just transported it."

"If you were smart enough to understand the math and other data, I'd show it to you."

"Transporting is still cool," Thatcher said.

"Fine, you're not a moron. I won't tell anyone."

"You can't. This is top-secret stuff, Thatch. If my dad or Jo ever find out—"

"I *said* I wouldn't tell anyone."

Eli seemed dubious, but he told Thatcher he was going to the bathroom and would put everything away when he got back.

Before the restroom door had even closed all the way, Thatcher opened the ship back up to peek inside again. He stuck his fist in, measuring, and then looked down at me. "Like it's made for you. Wanna take a ride?"

I did not want to take a ride. When he pulled his hand out, I ran. The room was large, but not large enough, and there were not enough things to hide behind. Thatcher chased me across the room and behind tables, my tiny legs no match for his long ones. He grabbed me by the scruff of my neck and shoved me into the egg, and when he slapped the side closed, the viewing screen popped on.

He had almost finished sequencing the launch when Eli came out of the restroom. He noticed my absence and just knew. Thatcher was taller and stronger, but Eli flew at him with his fist cocked back and hit him as hard as he could. It was only enough to make Thatcher stumble backward, so Eli hit him again and again until Thatcher crumbled to the floor.

As he fell, his hand slapped against the control panel, and the last thing I saw was Eli's horrified face, screaming "No!" as I launched.

That *No* echoed in Jo's office as Will turned the monitor off.

"I waited," he told them, moving from the back of the office. "Thatcher ran, and I waited there for hours, hoping that ship would return. I checked every day for weeks." He pulled the tablet from the docking port. "I recorded the launches we'd made, and any remote blip of data I found until I finally gave up. I knew it had probably gone off course and was lost somewhere and realized that it was Finn all over again. That ship was likely hundreds of years out of synch, and even if the cat inside survived, he wasn't coming home."

Curious, Jo asked, "Why didn't you tell someone?"

Eli dropped into the chair at Jo's desk. "Because there was no fixing this. My stupid ego had killed that innocent cat. What good would telling anyone do? It was my fault, and my guilt to live with."

It was why he quit. It was why he was so grumpy for the next year.

"I swore to myself I would never hurt anyone or anything again. But I could make them better. And I swear to god, I will. If I don't manage to survive med school, I'll find another way, but I *will* make it up to the universe somehow."

I jumped onto his lap and stretched up, my paws on his chest, and I touched my tongue to his chin.

"That's a kiss," Will murmured.

Tell him I know he fought Thatcher for me. I saw it. I'm not mad. I wanted to know how I started, and now I know.

"If I'd just left you in room seven," he sighed.

You didn't do this to me.

"But it's still my fault."

Eli picked me up and held me close, and when he spoke it was only to me. Will quietly repeated everything I said, because he knew it was just for Eli.

Okay. Then, thank you.

"How can you thank me, Wick? You were stuck for centuries."

I know. And then I became unstuck, and Will found me. He gave me cheese. Cheese, dude.

"And then he left you there. Wick, you were still a kitten when Thatcher shoved you into that ship."

We've always wondered why I stayed so small. Now we know. I went into null space when I was tiny. Time doesn't exist there, even though it also does. So I grew, but I didn't.

"But all those years..."

I don't think I'll try to remember them. Will found me, and I made him let me go. I was Seven, and I was Merlin, and then Major...it's been a good life. I was supposed to do all that so that I could be with my people.

"I'd still change it if I could."

Well, you could, but please don't. I don't belong in an office as someone's part-time pet. I belong with Will and Jax and Drew and Oz and Aubrey and Zed and Jay and Aisha and the newby. We're going to have a baby, dude. I wouldn't have any of this if I'd had to live my life as Seven, here in the office.

"My dad said he always suspected you had a big heart, Wick."

He's one of my favorite people. I can't wait until you're born. He's going to be so pissed off.

"Why?"

Because he wants a little girl. I'm going to mock him when you're born. A lot.

He hugged me, his breath moist on my ears. "I'm still sorry, Wick. I'm sorry for all the years you were alone and afraid. I own that sorrow, and I'll carry it with me."

It's okay. Is Jo really like your grandma, even though she's gonna be your daughter-in-law someday?

"She is, yes."

Then I'm stealing your grandma. That's how you make it all up to me. Let me take her home so she can get Luxor all fixed up, and then she can bounce around with Finn until she realizes that he's where she belongs. Maybe Will will finally get a little brother or sister.

"Oh, my god, Wick," Jo howled. "Do you have any idea how *old* we are?"

Do you have any idea how long Finn will live?

Will kept that to himself but reminded them that they were from a When where it was not outside the realm of possible. Not only could they still procreate, but he also wasn't so sure they weren't talking about it in his adopted When. It would be scandalous, a couple of people in their mid-70s having a baby, but he thought Jo might enjoy that.

"In any case," he added, "I would certainly enjoy that."

While they laughed about it, Drew sat quietly, staring at the monitor without really seeing it. He hadn't said a word, but stared ahead, his jaw set.

'He's quite upset,' Luxor said. *'Does he not like infants?'*

He loves babies. But I think his own just broke his heart.

"Not broken," Will said, reaching for me. "Give him a minute."

Eli swallowed hard. "Dad? Come on. Talk to me."

First, he sucked in a deep breath, and when he let it out, it was half sigh, half huff. "Fault or not, you were complicit in harming an *extremely* defenseless small animal. I'm disappointed in you for that, Eli. And I'm more disappointed that you didn't have the balls to be honest about it."

"What good would it—"

Quietly, evenly, Drew cut him off. "I thought I was raising a man who could own up to his mistakes, no matter how painful."

Get over it.

"Excuse me?" He snapped at Will because he thought that's who it came from, until Will pointed at me.

Get over it. He was fifteen. You were stupid when you were fifteen, too, I remember. And it's my life that was changed. I get to say if anyone gets upset.

"This goes beyond that," Drew insisted. "He betrayed Jo's trust by bringing Thatcher into the lab in the first place. He betrayed my trust—"

So? Get over it. You're going to in a little while anyway, so you might as well skip over the upset parts and get right to the forgiving parts.

"He's not wrong," Will said.

"Maybe he is, a bit," Eli said. "I'll earn your trust back, Dad. I swear."

You better tell him he already has it. Look what he's done. He left home to make sure someone else was okay. He grew up before he had to. He's the good man you raised, Drew. He made a mistake when he was a teenager and that's what being a teenager is for. If you can't be stupid when you're fifteen, when can you be? Besides, if you don't get over it, I'm telling Aubrey, and you know what she'll say? She'll say that you have to forgive him because if you don't, you'll make the baby Jesus cry. Blackshear men don't make the baby Jesus cry, Drew.

"Your cat," Drew said to Will, "is a pushy little f—"

"I am aware," Will said.

'Really, I have to go with these people?'
Trust me, Lux. You want to.

*

Oz—old Oz, this Drew's Oz—was waiting on Union Square when we returned. She hadn't expected to see Jo, so there was squealing and hugging, which made Luxor groan, though I suspect his indignity was manufactured for my benefit. Drew promised to explain it all to her, but he needed a good, stiff drink first.

That's how she knew it was serious.

Old Drew only drank on special occasions.

"It's a trial run," Jo told Oz, in answer to her surprise at seeing Jo again. "I know there's an age gap between us now, but if we can get past the hurt?"

"She says that now, but when she sees my apartment…" Finn smiled and shrugged. "I was going to get around to cleaning it one day."

"Yeah, and when was the last time you were even there?" Drew asked. "A year ago? Two?"

He wasn't sure.

"You're not taking her there," Oz insisted. "You're staying with us." When Jo started to balk, she added, "It's the family home. Finn is our grandson, no matter the When. You can stay in the guest room, live upstairs, or live downstairs, but you're not living in that hole he calls home but probably hasn't been to in a year or more."

"Imagine the smell, Mom," Will said. "Oz is saving you."

Lux, dude, there's a portal in the front bedroom closet.

Will, he needs a transponder.

"Let's get Luxor's heart taken care of before we worry about teaching him to time travel, all right?"

He said that, but I saw the light flash in Jo's eyes.

"Andrew." Will settled me onto his shoulder. "When you explain all of this to Oz, please don't forget the most important part—Wick would not change a thing. He quite firmly believes that he's entitled to every moment of his life, good or bad, and there should be no guilt, and absolutely no repercussions."

"You're a good man, Wick," Drew said.

I know. One thing.

Does anyone know what happened to that Thatcher kid?

"Angus Thatcher?" Oz asked. "Eli's old friend?"

"He died when they were seventeen," Drew said. "They hadn't been friends for a long time, and now we know why. But he was killed during a robbery gone horrifically wrong."

That sucks. I mean, he was a tool, but it still sucks.

"Funny enough," Finn said, "he was the victim, not the perpetrator. And he died protecting a total stranger."

"But god, that kid was an ass," Oz sighed.

Drew reached for her hand. "Ozzy, you have no idea."

"Coming in for a drink, Emperor?" Oz asked. "Drew seems to need one. You can stay the night and spend some time with Jo and Finn if you like. We have plenty of room."

Will was torn. He wanted to stay there with Finn and Jo, to find a way to make sure that she stayed, but every day he stayed was a day off his life, a day he could spend with Aisha. I perched on his shoulder while he hugged them, trying to not dig my claws into him, ignoring Luxor as he sat on the ground mocking me for my grace, or lack thereof. Will hugged Finn first, and whispered into his ear, "Don't screw this up, Dad. You have a younger, hotter wife now. Make her want to stay."

Jo heard it and snickered under her breath, and when he went to hug her, she said, "Don't worry so much. And I was hot before, dammit."

He pulled back to look at her. "Ah, you're my mother. Your degree of hotness isn't something I generally contemplate."

But hers is.

He kissed Jo on the forehead and then looked up. She was crossing the Square, walking deliberately toward him, every bit as light in her step as she'd been several decades earlier. She also seemed a bit uncertain, as if he might not want to see much less speak to her. That didn't stop her; she kept her eyes on his as the distance between them closed, and she exhaled a sorrow-tinged sigh when she stopped only a few feet away.

His shoulder tightened under me; this woman had lived through the death of the Emperor. While they weren't speaking when that happened, she surely knew, and he was at a loss about what to say to her.

"Don't go running off," she said when he couldn't get anything out. "I won't bite."

Finn scooped Lux up, and they all stepped away.

"Right here," she said to him. "Almost sixty years ago, we were standing right here when you broke my heart and then ran away."

Dude...

Will had no idea what to say. She shouldn't recognize him for who he was. She should have thought he was a distant relative who happened to look like the young man who abruptly ended things so many years before. He opened his mouth to speak, but nothing came out.

"I know that it's you, Emperor." She tilted her head a touch and smiled. "You shaved. I don't like it."

That made him laugh. "How?"

"How could I not recognize you?" She tapped a finger to the side of her head. "You never left here. You're a bastard, but you never left."

She could have called him every horrible name off Aubrey's list, and he would have happily stood there and listened, just to hear her voice.

No one else existed for him. He gestured to the closest table at a snack stand, one that used to be the little bakery, and asked her to sit with him for a few minutes. She walked ahead of him, and he took in every detail he could; she was nearly 80 years old but hadn't gone gray, and she moved with grace, not the elderly shuffle one might expect.

Finn brushed past, deftly handing Will his cash card, and told him they'd catch up later.

"My son," she finally told him after he went in and got coffee and hot chocolate. "He and Zed are still very close. Drunk men talk. And then hungover men have to prove the things they boasted about when they were drunk."

She'd known for years about the portals. Zed had even taken Jimmy, who was not Jay in this When, through a few times, usually to sit at Sophia's café with coffee and wishes, because Zed felt closest to her there, in the early days of their life together, when it was her passion. He was careful to not cross paths with her but was certain she'd spotted him a time or two.

It was after Jax's 80th birthday that Zed came clean with her, with the few details he felt comfortable enough telling her. At first, she thought it was wishful thinking; maybe he'd visited the past in years when the Emperor was still alive and allowed himself to think it was true. But he was so earnest, swearing that the Emperor had been there for Jax's birthday, that she allowed herself to hope he was telling the complete truth.

"I went to your funeral, Emperor. I saw your father and King Eli nearly come to blows over you. And yet there I was, believing that you'd somehow survived."

"That Emperor did die," he said, gently. "My presence here doesn't erase that reality. I'm simply the one from the next loop of time, and in that one, my life is spared."

Her hand twitched toward him.

"How much did Zed tell you about me?" he asked.

"Not enough. I still don't know your name. More importantly, I don't know why you left." She shifted, holding her cup close to her face, letting the steam brush across her nose. "I was angry for a long time. Don't let my demeanor fool you. But I want answers, even now."

This is your birthday party all over again.
Touch her. Show her why.

He leaned back, folding his arms, trying to not grin too hard. "First, tell me this much. Have you been happy? Had the life you wanted?"

Dude, you know that.

"I've had the life I chose to have," she answered simply.

"I hope it's been happy."

"Did you ever look me up?" she wondered out loud. "Poked around online to find out what I was doing? I had the luxury of seeing you in the news and on gossip sites. You seemed happy, which both irritated the hell out of me and gave me a tiny bit of peace."

"I wanted to. I nearly caved into the temptation a few thousand times."

"Yet, you didn't."

"My heart wouldn't have been able to take it if I'd learned something had happened to you."

I hopped off his shoulder and walked across the table to her. *He's an idiot. Make him tell you the truth. He already knows about your life. He snooped.*

She reached out to pet me. "He's so tiny."

"And mouthy."

"He looks like—" She had to stop to think about it, trying to fish me out of the recesses of her brain. "You and Jax carried a tiny thing around with you nearly everywhere. He lived with Jax, but I always felt like he was yours. This little guy looks just like him."

"Wick," he said. "And there's a reason for that."

"Come on."

He held his hand out to her. "I can explain it all. And hopefully, you'll take it as well as you did a year ago, when you waltzed into my birthday party, walked up to me, and said, 'You broke my heart, Emperor.'" When she stared at his hand, he added, "You can touch me. But fair warning, you won't expect the results."

"If this had happened sixty years ago," she sighed.

"This will explain why I didn't touch anyone back then, I hope."

It took longer this time. At his birthday party, she'd accepted it easily; this time she squeezed her eyes closed, and when she pulled her hand back, she didn't look up. Even after she opened her eyes, she didn't look up. She stared at the table, and then at his hand.

"You married." She touched a finger to the ring on his finger. "All the years I followed you in the news, no one ever mentioned—"

"Newly married," he said. "Less than a year."

You didn't tell her that much? Are you insane?

Finally, she looked up. "You didn't bat an eye when I said that my son and Zed were still close friends. You never knew that Jimmy was my son. I was so careful to make sure you never connected us."

"I learned that at my party." He sighed happily. "It was a wonderful birthday. I danced with the most beautiful woman in Pacifica that night." He waited a beat and said, "Stubborn woman, she is. Made me apologize for my behavior two decades earlier. And when we danced? While I was still out of my mind with joy that this woman was finally in my arms, even if I did wear gloves to protect her thoughts, she learned that I'd never been kissed."

Her eyes flashed, understanding.

"By then she understood what can happen when I touch someone. Yet she came straight out and asked me if it was worth the risk, and then didn't really wait for me to answer. Even if it had ended there, if she had left the party and refused to ever see me again, I think that would wind up being the most memorable kiss of anyone's life."

"My turn, then," she said. "Are you happy?"

"Happy doesn't begin to scratch the surface."

They talked for a long time. The others had gone home, but every now and then I saw someone peek over the balcony to snoop. He peppered her with questions about her life and her work, and he gave evasive answers about himself. He never said outright that she was the one who had given him his first kiss, nor that they'd married. He made sure she understood that was what had happened, though, and that he would turn back the clock for her if he could.

Without saying the words, he made sure she knew that the boy who had left her heartbroken on Union Square so many decades ago had lied when he said he didn't love her. He handed the truth to her, that even had her Emperor lived, it was the right thing to do, because it gave the world Jimmy Okuda, and the world needed him.

Before they parted, she reached over and touched his hand and said, "Be gentle with her son, Emperor. He has a hard road ahead. Maybe you can make it a little easier."

Oh my cod, tell her!

She needed to leave; he stood to help her and didn't pull back when it was clear she wasn't ready to let go of his hand.

"I still don't know your name. And don't tell me it really is 'Emperor.'"

"William. Will. Blackshear."

"So, you really were related to Jax." She let go of his hand and patted him on the chest. "I wondered, from time to time."

"People do," he admitted.

"Brothers?"

"No. We're distantly related."

"More secrets. All right. Then tell me, Will, is it still worth the risk?"

He had no idea what she meant until her hand slid to his neck and she leaned forward and kissed him.

"She'll forgive you," she said as she began walking away, "because I was owed that kiss."

"Aisha." He took one step toward her, stopping when she looked over her shoulder. "That was just as memorable."

"Oh, hon, I damn well know that."

13

He held onto Aisha so long that people on Union Square were snickering about it. No one pointed and laughed, but they noticed and found it funny. Or touching. It could have been either. They didn't care what anyone else thought, and Will had been away just long enough to miss her more than a tiny bit. To her, he'd been gone no longer than it took to walk from the apartment to the Square, but she soaked up every second of that hug like it was cool water straight from a newly opened can of tuna.

After he hugged her, he kissed her. By the time that was over, Finn and Jo—our Finn and Jo, Will's actual, directly in line parents—had come up from the lab and Aubrey and Jax had chosen right then to go for a walk, which they rarely did because it meant dragging guards along and inconveniencing the masses. But it was a nice day, and they decided that the people could stand the inconvenience for an hour.

We sat at a table at the little corner bakery on the Square, while Will told them everything except for their future grandson's name. He managed to relate it all without a hint of how old Eli was, or even his gender, which annoyed Jax enough that he threatened to issue a royal decree requiring Will to eat a dozen donuts dripping with sugar and chocolate.

Will was not a fan of sweet things, but he accepted the risk and reminded Jax that the future was fluid, and the grandchildren he got might not be the same.

You might have a puppy. That's what he told Drew.

"You truly don't want to know what happened in the years you don't recall?" Aubrey picked me up and kissed my head, right between my ears, because she knew I liked it when she did that. "San Francisco has a colorful history, and you might have been a major part of that."

I know how I began. That's what I wanted.

And now I'll always remember Tad. He was the hero of my hardest years. He protected me and cared for me even when he couldn't take me home.

And I'll always remember that Will gave me my first taste of cheese, and promised me he would give me more, for the rest of my life.

"I gave you ham, too, yet you fixated on that cheese."

Cheese is cheese. Of course, I did.

"Any idea whatever happened to Tad?" Aisha asked. "He spent so many years looking after Wick, and now I feel like I need to know."

I don't even know his last name.

"Thaddeus Mackenzie," Finn said. "I was curious. Will knew the name of his mother's shop, so it wasn't a stretch to follow the crumbs. He went to UC in Davis, studied veterinarian medicine, and then specialized in small animal care in a little suburb of Sacramento. There's an old website dedicated to his memory, started by his grandchildren. I mean, it's been dormant since the late twenty-first century, but it's a reasonably detailed biography of the man. He apparently spent his birthday every year in San Francisco, and—I quote—he was 'looking for the magic.'"

Merlin. He kept looking for Merlin.

"There's no way he could have guessed how long Wick would live," Jax said.

Aubrey didn't think he really expected to find me. His heart needed to be there, and after some time it was probably a tradition he didn't want to lose. "How sad that he never knew his Merlin found a forever home, though."

"Perhaps he should get some closure," Will said. "How detailed was that website, Dad?"

Finn pulled a tablet out of his backpack and turned it on, handing it to Will after the site had loaded. Will was quiet for a long time, reading about the life of Tad, the first person other than Will to care for me after I'd fallen from null space, through the stars, and into the city. Everyone else carried on a conversation that was nothing more than a buzz in his ears, and they talked until the coffee was cold and the temperature began to drop.

When he was done, he sighed and then turned the tablet off. "One more quick trip, Wick?"

Are we going to Sacramento?

"No. We're going to twenty-thirty, right here in San Francisco. Tad died at the med center. He was eighty years old."

He went home to change; I could hide in the jacket Mrs. Kovlov had made for our trip to the nineteen-sixties, and Tad might remember it. He grabbed cash for that When, in case he needed to bribe someone to get into Tad's room or take a taxi around town, and Finn offered to go with us, to stand as a lookout.

"You never know, Dash. I've been in those old hospitals. If I stand outside his door looking appropriately upset, anyone intending on going in to check on him will wait."

He just wants to go somewhere with you. Let him come.

Both Aubrey and Jo reminded them to be careful, because that's what moms do, and when Aisha got up to kiss him, she tugged on the front of his jacket and said, "Last trip for a while, all right? Unless Jax needs you for something, can we make this the final one until after the baby gets here?"

He was willing to wait until then for this. It didn't matter if we went now or a year from now, but she wanted him to get it over with.

"Do this for Wick. I bet he needs closure, too."

Until that came out of her mouth, I hadn't realized the truth of it. I needed to see Tad and to thank him for saving my life. Even if he didn't remember me, if age and time had plucked me like fruit from his tree of memories, I needed to thank him. I wanted him to know, in case it mattered to him, that he had been a good man even when he was a little boy. Whatever else life had thrown at him after he was fifteen and moved away, he'd been a good man when I needed one in my life.

We went through the portal on Union Square and arrived in the middle of the night. There were more people than I expected to see after midnight, but no one paid any attention to us. We walked past bars and clubs illuminated by bright pseudo-neon signs along the way to the hospital, crossing the street once to avoid a homeless guy defecating on the sidewalk, and no one looked either Will or Finn in the eyes.

Before we turned the corner to the front side of the hospital, we passed a young woman who sat on the sidewalk with her knees bent to her chest and her arms wrapped tightly around them. She rocked back and forth, swaying to the music inside her own head, and she muttered, "I'm not high, I'm not high, I'm not high," over and over. She was still locked into that quiet chant when we reached the door and went inside.

I wanted to tell Will to turn around and go help her, but I knew what the answer would be. I also knew it tore at him to leave her there, because she wasn't any older than Jay and she was most certainly high, and probably had no idea what she'd taken.

Tad was in a room on the third floor. The walls

of the halls we walked were screaming bright white decorated with long swirls of blue paint, and the air stung my nose. Every room we passed screamed in beeps and squeals, the sounds of hearts beating, and air being forced into lungs too tired to do it on their own anymore.

Finn found the room, just inside the double-doored entry to the oncology unit. It was far from the nurse's station, and there were no security guards in sight, but Finn said he would wait outside just in case. If a nurse or doctor looked like they were coming in, he would knock gently.

Will wasn't worried. The worst that could happen was that we'd be asked to leave.

He hoped.

Old Tad was thin and hairless, his skin hanging from tired bones in wafer-like folds. He had his own beeping machines, but he was breathing on his own and slept with his upper body at a slight incline. Will watched him sleep for a minute, making sure it was just sleep and not something deeper, and then he set his hand on Tad's bare chest.

It was kinder and quieter to wake him up with a gentle thought inside his own head. Will whispered to him that he had visitors, and to trust what he saw with his own eyes. Tad's breath deepened, and his eyes fluttered open, the wetness in them gleaming in the light that filtered in through the window.

"I brought someone to see you," Will whispered. His hand was still on Tad's chest, feeding him memories of birthdays spent chasing down a frightened little cat in the aquatic park, and the times he'd run into Will. "I know you worried about him when you moved."

He pulled me out of his jacket pocket and set me on Tad's chest.

Tad's voice was a thread of air. He struggled, waving at the controller by his head; he wanted to sit up a bit more to see me better. But he managed one word, and it was enough that I knew he believed.

"Merlin."

As his hand went to my back, he looked up at Will, his eyes asking the question he couldn't get out his mouth: How?

"It's complicated," Will said. "But yes, this is Merlin. My father picked him up after you moved. He's had a very good life. And a long one."

Show him. Tonight is his last night. Let him see.

"I can show you the life he's led, Tad. I would need to touch you again, and you would see the images in your mind. It's much easier to show you than to tell you, and I promise, it won't hurt."

He breathed, "Merlin," again, and grabbed Will's hand and set it back on his chest, right next to me. His eyes closed, and I stretched to get a paw on his skin so that I could see, too. Will showed him everything; my first taste of cheese, all the birthdays when Will showed up to sit on the bleachers, and he let Tad peek at the cat in his jacket and let him hear the conversations we had with Merlin. He took Tad through our lives together, when we realized we could speak to each other, and when Finn took me to Jax. He saw my life unfold, and how happy it was with all the people who loved me.

In a few minutes, Will gave him a lifetime of memories.

"He'd have had none of that, if not for you," Will said. "He was close to dying when you began feeding him. Your generosity gave him decades that he wouldn't have had."

Will turned his head a touch, listening as Tad spoke to him. His lips never moved, but he'd opened his eyes and stared right into Will's.

"Yes, he knew you didn't want to leave him behind. He never blamed you. He's grateful."

Tell him I thought he was magnificent. And fantastic. And I'm proud of him. Remind him that he was a good man, even when he was nine.

The rest of the conversation was silent; I pulled my paw back so I could creep closer to his face and gently headbutt his chin. I sat up when Will finally pulled his hand away, but he didn't stand up straight. He kept his face close to Tad's, and said, "I know quite a bit about you, and I promise, Wick's not lying. For all of your days, you were a good man."

With a gentle touch to his forehead, Will put him back to sleep, to savor the memories he'd been given as the last dreams of his life.

Will was quiet on the walk to the front door of the hospital, but when we were outside, he sucked down a deep breath and said, "He needed that, Wick."

"How much longer does he have?" Finn asked.

"He'll pass away in his sleep just before dawn. He's ready. He's tired of fighting and wants to join his wife in the next life."

Is there a next life?

"More and more, I think Aubrey is right, Wick. There has to be something else. I desperately want there to be, because even a hundred years with Aisha won't be enough."

*

In a way, perhaps a roundabout way, Will needed closure as much as I did. He needed to know how I started, and he needed to thank Tad for caring for me. Tad was the gentle capstone to too many years of misery for me, and while he wished I hadn't had to endure that last year without him, Will was as sure as I was that if not for Tad, I might not have trusted Finn enough to allow him to pick me up to take me home.

But there was something else, something just for him. He needed closure for the Aisha who had lost her Emperor; it was something he had often wrestled with when visiting old Jax and old Aubrey, whether to seek her out and tell her or leave it alone. He'd thought it might be crueler than kind because she didn't know about time travel and the portals and how Oz and Drew's lives especially had woven through so many Whens.

He eventually decided that telling her would be a slap in the face. Presenting himself was divulging that the life she'd wanted was there, just not for her.

When she made her way across Union Square and knew who he was, he expected fury. He'd been willing to stand there and take in every anger-laced expletive she had for him and apologize as many times as it took, and still expected no forgiveness. Yet deep down he knew that if that happened, it wouldn't last. Her curiosity would outweigh the upset, he was sure of that.

"Her life was good," he told Aisha. "Whatever anger she held toward me had faded with time. She's still involved in a wonderful career and bubbles with excitement when she talks about her son. I must admit, it did my heart good to see her so happy."

We were on the balcony; Jay and Zed were down on Union Square with Zara and Sophia, waiting for Oz and Drew. They had asked to borrow Will's car to go to Ocean Beach for an evening picnic, and when it was too cold, they planned on ending the day at a dessert bar near Golden Gate Park. Because they were in public, Will didn't feel as if it was snooping to watch them while they waited, and Aisha didn't care. She loved seeing them all together, snooping or not.

"I think I would have had a great life even if I hadn't worked up the nerve to go to your party last year," she said. "I'd have traveled the world and had boy toys in all the major metropolitan cities.

And here I am now, chained to this gorgeous man, and I'm going to get *so* fat in a few months."

He didn't care how big she got; she was going to be the most beautiful person he could ever hope to set eyes on. "And perhaps not so surprising, she did travel quite a bit."

"And the boy toys?" she teased.

"I did not inquire. But one might assume." He reached for her hand. "At the risk of bolstering an unfair stereotype...I don't see that woman as having been alone for any length of time. I would imagine that even at her age she does not lack for companionship."

"And you aren't the least bit biased, are you?"

"Ask Wick," he said, laughing. "He'll be honest. You are going to be a smoking hot eighty-year-old."

That got him a kiss.

Oh! Tell her! Tell her you kissed another woman!

If you don't, I'll tell Drew, and he'll tell her. So she's gonna find out. Tell her!

"Are you spilling secrets, Wick?" she asked me.

I just want him to tell the truth. He cheated on you!

"I did not cheat on her," he grumbled.

"What'd you do, Will?" She sounded amused, not upset, though she gave him a side look that made him think twice about it.

"It's not what *I* did. However, before she left, she kissed me, and I did nothing to stop her."

On the lips!

"What are talking? Peck on the cheek? Grabbed you and threw you into a dip? Sucked the enamel off your teeth?"

He leaned over and kissed her, sweetly, and then said, "Quite a bit like that. And I won't lie, I enjoyed it."

"So did I. Kiss me like that again."

He's not stupid; he kissed her again. And just as they parted, Drew called out from the entryway, "Why the hell is there a strange white cat in our room?"

Lux!

"Seriously," Drew said as we went back inside, "I was sitting on the edge of the bed tying my shoes, and this...cat...popped out of the closet."

Move so I can go see him. You're blocking my way.

"I can explain," Will started. Oz came out holding Lux, scratching his head between his ears. "Clearly, he's not hurting anyone."

"Yet," Drew grumbled.

"His name is Luxor. He belongs to my mother."

"Jo got a cat?" Oz asked.

'Ask her to put me down. She's nice, but I'm not ready to be this familiar with her.'

"He wants down," Drew told her. "When did Jo get a cat?"

Will's eyebrows twitched. "Did you understand him?"

"He wanted down, right?"

"Wick?" Will asked me.

He wanted down.

Luxor sat next to me and looked up at Drew. *'Who are you? You smell familiar.'*

"I'm Drew. Who are you?"

'This is Drew? My Drew? And he can understand me?'

"Will someone explain what the hell is going on?" Drew asked.

Luxor is Jo's cat thirty years from now.

"And that makes perfect sense. Will?"

Will gestured to the living room, promising an explanation. Aubrey was in the kitchen, so I nudged Lux in that direction, and we jumped on the counter so that he could introduce himself. She didn't even flinch, she just smiled and said, "Well, hello there. Who are you?"

"His name is Luxor," Oz called from the living room. "He's Jo's cat in about thirty years, and he came to visit Wick."

"How fun." She greeted him with a kiss on his head and then had one for me. "Wick, you should introduce him to Jax. He's in the bedroom, reading. I think he'd enjoy meeting Luxor."

Oz chuckled, and as we headed for the bedroom, I heard her say, "That's a little evil, Mom."

We sprinted down the hall. Luxor's long legs meant he got there first, and when he did he leaped at Jax from halfway across the room and landed cleanly in his lap. To his credit, Jax didn't panic and toss Lux to the floor, but shouted out, "What the hell?!"

Lux, meet Jax. He's the King, and he's Finn's great-grandfather.

'He startles easily.'

You have no idea. I surprise him with my hover cart a lot. Zoom right toward his face at five in the morning when he's only half awake. He screams like a little girl.

'You have your own hover cart?'

It was my birthday present last year. I'll let you ride it before you go home.

Aubrey came in to explain who Luxor was, and then said he was staying for a visit, so Jax might as well get used to a second cat. She also said she'd put down a snack for us, so we headed back to the kitchen, and when we were done eating, Luxor cleaned his whiskers and his paws, very deliberately and delicately.

'I was supposed to say hello and then go right home.'

Time travel, dude. Leave tonight, leave tomorrow, leave next week. You'll still go right back home.

He wanted to stay for a while and especially wanted to meet younger Jo.

I wanted him to really meet Oz and Drew.

'Where's Eli?' Lux wanted to know.

Not born yet. That's still a few years away. Oh, and don't tell Drew about Eli. All of that is supposed to be a surprise.

When we went back to the living room, Lux jumped on the coffee table to sniff them, rubbing against Oz's fingers when she held her hand out to him. "Look at his eyes, Drew. I've never seen eyes so blue. Lux, you are a gorgeous little man."

'I'm not little but thank you. Your appearance is quite pleasant, as well.'

"Well, now," she said when the translation worked its way around to her, "you're definitely welcome to stay a while."

"How's your heart, Luxor?" Will asked. "Are you doing all right?"

'I'm well, thank you. My heart has been repaired, and Jo is quite thankful that Wick was able to help me.'

Will's going to want to know about her and Finn. Did she stay?

'She stayed. We live upstairs from Oz and Drew now, but I am allowed to move freely in the building.'

Will leaned forward to give Lux a head rub. "You can't tell Drew anything about his life there, all right?"

'I know. He needs to be surprised.' He reached a paw out and touched Drew's knee. *'Could I trouble you to show me where the litter box is?'*

While Drew led him down the hall, I jumped into Will's lap and stretched up to give his chin a tiny lick.

I have a friend, Will. A real friend.

"I know. I'm very happy for you. I hope he can visit often."

Can I visit him?

"I don't imagine I could stop you. But yes, I don't see why not. All I ask is that you tell me when you're going and that you don't stay there more than a day or two. We'll send Lux home tomorrow, all right? This first visit should be short."

Okay.

Are you happy? She stayed with Finn.

"Very happy, Wick. But what matters most to me is that they're happy together."

'They laugh a lot,' Lux said from the hallway. *'They dance in the living room in the evening and muse that the only thing missing is a little boy hiding behind the chair, watching them.'*

"I never knew they'd spotted me there."

'Please visit them soon. It's only been a few weeks, but she needs to see you.'

Aisha reached over and rubbed his arm. "I know I asked you to stay until the baby comes, but if you need to go—"

"They can come here. We'll figure it out." He gestured to Lux and me. "We have messengers now."

'They don't understand me.'

He can clip a note to your collar. Or he can clip one to mine. I know how to get there.

Oz and Drew had to leave—Zed and Jay were still waiting for them—and Jax came out of the bedroom to get a better look at Lux. He crouched in front of the coffee table and apologized for being less than welcoming in the bedroom. "I was caught by surprise, but it was rude, and I'm sorry. I'm happy to meet you and hope that you have fun during your visit. In fact, I think Wick needs to show you his hover cart tonight. Will and Aisha have a nice, long hallway that would be perfect for your first ride on it."

"Let me guess," Will said. "You think they should play with it at four in the morning."

"Three, four, their choice."

'They're a little bit evil, aren't they?'

They like to pick on each other.

'I like that. I think I'm going to enjoy this visit.'

I led the way to the staircase so that I could show him the hover cart, and as we made our way up I heard Will sigh and then tell Aisha, "Why do I have a feeling those two are the trouble twins?"

"Well, Wick *was* testing you last fall to make sure you were ready for parenthood," she said. "Maybe this is the final exam."

She wasn't wrong.

Four-forty-five in the morning, on his way out to meet Jax for their morning run, Will would get his cumulative grade. It all depended on how many words he rattled from the Bad Word List, if he screamed louder than Jax, and whether he got angry when Lux aimed straight for his face while I bolted between his legs or if he just ducked and kept going.

I wasn't too worried.

I planned on grading on a curve.

ABOUT THE AUTHOR
BECAUSE PEOPLE TOTALLY READ THIS STUFF WHEN THEY'RE DONE READING
THE BOOK

Max Thompson is a writer living in Northern California with The Woman, The Man, and Buddah Pest. He's also a Feline Life Coach for Mousebreath Magazine, and writes the hugely popular blog *The Psychokitty Speaks Out*. He's 14 pounds of sleek black and white feline glory, and his favorite snacks are real live fresh dead steak, shrimp, and lots of cheese. He also appreciates that you've read this far, and would give you a cookie if he could.